Rupture

Rupture

Stories on the Sorrows of Kashmir

RATTAN LAL SHANT

Translated and Edited by
DR JAVAID IQBAL BHAT

OXFORD
UNIVERSITY PRESS

Great Clarendon Street, Oxford, ox2 6dp,
United Kingdom

Oxford University Press is a department of the University of Oxford.
It furthers the University's objective of excellence in research, scholarship,
and education by publishing worldwide. Oxford is a registered trade mark of
Oxford University Press in the UK and in certain other countries

First Edition published in 2022

Published in the United States of America by Oxford University Press
198 Madison Avenue, New York, NY 10016, United States of America

British Library Cataloguing in Publication Data

Data available

Library of Congress Control Number: 2022934899

ISBN 978–0–19–286508–3

DOI: 10.1093/oso/9780192865083.001.0001

Endorsements

'Rattan Lal Shant's at once subtle and powerful portrayal of the tragedy of Kashmir comes alive in Javaid Iqbal Bhat's sensitive translation.'

—Ira Raja, Professor of English, University of Delhi

'Steeped in the beauty of the land, it brings out poetic pathos. The cultural landscape that breathes through the vivid imagery elevates the story. One finds a sense of nostalgia woven with the longing of the nation.'

—Saba Mahmood Bashir, Assistant Professor, Department of English, Jamia Millia Islamia

For all those hundreds of unknown people
who
Gave their life to guard those testimonies
Which for eternity will keep on showing
There was connection before separation.

Foreword

A large number of books have been written about Kashmir in the recent past.

Modern Kashmir has in fact been a writers' paradise. The situation in Kashmir was not normal, in the conventional sense of that word, ever since the Partition of the subcontinent. However, the situation turned worse from the early 1990s onwards with the social and economic fabric coming under intense strain. The turbulence which ensued spawned a huge publishing industry. Most of these books are written by non-Kashmiris not equipped with the lived experience of the situation. And most of them used political registers to inscribe their thoughts, given the charged political atmosphere of Kashmir. Hence there are books about the political genesis of the conflict, implications of the political conflict especially the human suffering consequent upon the rise of the conflict, contentious arguments and counter-arguments about a particular nationalistic position. In the process an entire library has come up for study. A primer on Kashmir, for a newcomer, might include scores of books to eventually make their way into almost nowhere. A maze of narratives has been created, in which the reader feels lost for direction. However, this book meets the promise of taking the reader out of the maze.

The collection of stories titled *Rupture* is, in form and substance, a different narrative from the ones mentioned earlier. Away from the 'superficial' take of sociopolitical narratives, *Rupture* probes into the lives of people and explores the fabric which began to fray at the edges and is now in tatters. As I moved from one story to another story, I could feel the temper and tone of people and the texture of the multi-coloured fabric caught up in the vortex of this never-ending conflict. The web of conflict is such that hardly any community has been left untouched. Both Muslims and Hindus feel trapped and helpless, without any sign of hope in the future. The unremitting suffering is a common thread weaving its way into the fabric of this collection. An uninitiated reader will be taken into an entirely different space and time of loss and mourning for a place which, in the superficial imagination of people, is ridiculously identified with unearthly paradise, ignoring the blood and gore which has been the hallmark of the lives of all communities.

The calm and composed short stories, written against the background of migration of Hindus from Kashmir, compel a rethink on the modern outlook on Kashmir.

There is somewhat of a pattern in these short stories. A good number of them have been written before the migration of Kashmiri Hindus from Kashmir to different parts of India. Others have been written after their migration. A strand which stands out is the nostalgia for the inter-community bonhomie before the migration. There are some stories which delineate the beautifully entangled lives of Hindus and Muslims before the turbulent years of early 1990s. The post-migration stories mourn the loss of home, and the intensification of belonging for the culture and material objects back in Kashmir. In one of the stories, an elderly pandit woman has managed to take her local god in the box when her family had to suddenly leave home for Jammu. Her dream is to make a temple near the refugee camp in Jammu and install the god in that temple, for which purpose she is very passionate and mobilizes her meagre family resources. She wants to sacralize the refugees and the refugee camp, the way Kashmir was in the past. There is an elderly pandit man who had spent most of his life in Kashmir, and is now suddenly forced to live in the refugee camp, and what he does often is to move from one place to another in the courtyard, lost in his own world, unmindful of what others are thinking of him. Some characters do muster the courage of going back to Kashmir briefly, but only find themselves witnessing the misery of Muslim neighbours and their old homes reduced to mounds of un-attended earth for children to play. The point is it takes a lot of courage to return, even briefly, to a home lost to the misfortune of time. Among other things, what stand out are the cramped spaces of refugees, little rooms with abysmal government support in the form of food and hygiene. The refugee emerges some kind of a wanderer, both in body and in imagination.

Rattan Lal Shant is a native Kashmiri, well-versed with the history and culture of Kashmir. I am not familiar with the Kashmiri language, but from what I could gather from the translation, it is clear to me that Mr Shant has brought to bear his deep knowledge and intimate experience of life in Kashmir and outside (as a refugee) upon these stories. The characters, events, and stories breathe out the rich recesses of the inter-religious relationships. There seems to be little rancour and bitterness, and more of a desire for mutual inter-religious peaceful cohabitation in his literary imagination. These stories will draw the reader away from the official descriptions of 'heaven' and 'paradise' into a world of ruptures, gaps, silences, and alleys of desolation. These are stories of could-have-been paradise which unfortunately is riven by suspicion and instability. The collection is an elegy to a land which has rich cultural and intellectual roots; a land which nurtured the roots of classical Sanskrit learning and watered the Persian literature, establishing sound connections with the intellectual orbits of these two classical languages. One can only hope that the antique atmosphere of tranquillity and peace will return one day and usher in a fresh era in which modern Abhinavguptas and Ghani Kashmiris will take birth.

And finally, I have had the opportunity of teaching Dr Javaid Iqbal Bhat while he was an MA student in the Center for English Studies, Jawaharlal Nehru University. During the four years of his stay at the center, I saw him grow intellectually and developing a more mature and serious outlook on life. He was one of my most serious students, who had spent his childhood in Kashmir, and witnessed the mayhem and disorder first hand. I believe he has the requisite skill, experience, and sensitivity in translating the mood and content of these stories. And he has actually succeeded in that. Any reader interested in the cultural climate of migrated Kashmiri Hindus will not be disappointed after reading these stories.

Professor Kapil Kapoor
Chairman, Indian Institute of Advanced Studies

Acknowledgements

The translation of a text is mostly a solitary endeavour. This work is no exception. However, there are many people without whose moral and literary support this translation would not have reached completion. Many people came forward and assisted me to complete this project.

At the outset, I am thankful to Prof. Rattan Lal Talashi, former Professor, Department of Kashmiri, University of Kashmir, for reposing trust in me to translate these short stories. The translation work of this collection took off after I received the book from him. This project would have remained incomplete without his practical suggestions from time to time. He was always there available to answer any query. I am also thankful to Prof. Rattan Lal Shant, the original author, for permitting me to translate and publish the stories.

My thanks also go to Dr Nisar Nadeem, Assistant Professor, Dept. of Kashmiri, Government Degree College (Boys) Anantnag, Kashmir. I am immensely grateful for his time and valuable assistance. He was easily available in his office in college and also on phone, whenever I felt the need.

My sincere thanks to Mr Iftikhar Imran, Lecturer, Dept. of English, Higher Secondary School, Kargil for copy-editing the translation. He had a close look at the manuscript and aided in improving the quality of syntax.

I deeply appreciate Mr Ghulam Nabi Aatash, former Lecturer and a Sahitya Akademi awardee, for his advice and assistance, and in unravelling some tales and myths which form the context of some of the stories. Despite being bed-ridden for some time, he was ever ready and cheerful in extending his support. He is an inspiring literary person, in addition to being a good host.

I am thankful to Prof. Ishfaq, Assistant Professor, Dept. of Kashmiri, Govt. Womens' College, Anantnag for his help whenever required.

I am indebted to Dr Shafkat Altaf, Sr. Asst. Prof., Dept. of Kashmir, University of Kashmir, for several long telephonic conversations I had with him about the content and ethnic context of the original text. His experience in translating texts came in handy.

I extend my thanks to Mr Hriday Kaul Bharti, who, on some occasions told me the subtle and hidden meanings of some words that are particular to some rituals and customs of Kashmiri pandits. He threw light on some customs and rituals native to the Kashmiri pandit community.

Mr Barakat Ali, former Professor, Dept. of Kashmir, Govt. Womens' College, Anantnag chipped in at times. Mr Sabzar Ahmad, research scholar, Dept. of Kashmiri, University of Kashmir was also helpful on some occasions. Dr Shahida Shabnam, Assistant Professor, Dept. of Kashmiri, Govt. College Sopore also helped reshape some lines and words in translation. Thanks to all of them.

I am grateful to Dr Iffat Maqbool, Sr. Assistant Prof., Dept. of English, University of Kashmir, for editing a story, and setting the right tone and style for editing the rest of the translation.

Last but not the least, I owe a great deal to my family for bearing with my absence from routine family work. I especially thank my father for instilling and encouraging my interest in reading and writing. He saw me start this work but could not survive until its completion.

Contents

Rattan Lal Shaant

Bio-Note (Translated from the blurb of the book)

Rattan Lal Shaant was born in Srinagar on 14 May 1938. He did BA from University of Kashmir and MA and DPhil from Allahabad University. From 1959 to 1996 he taught Hindi and Kashmiri languages and literature in different colleges of Kashmir and for a short time in University of Kashmir. He wrote his first short story in 1953. Up to now he has published four collections of short stories, two critical texts on short stories, and three translations. In addition to that he has published eight texts in Hindi. He wrote many critical essays on some issues of poetry, culture, and language in Kashmiri, Hindi, Urdu, and English. He has written four dozen dramas for radio and television. He edited some journals and presented some dramas. He received awards like President's Gold medal, Nehru Award, prize from Ministry of Human Resources, from Uttar Pradesh Government, millennium award, and Jammu and Kashmir Cultural Academy award.

Translator Bio-Note

Javaid Iqbal Bhat has done his PhD from Ohio University, USA. He is working as an Assistant Professor in the Department of English, South Campus, University of Kashmir. He has completed his Master of English and Master of Philosophy Programs from the Center for English Studies, Jawaharlal Nehru University, Delhi. He specializes in Literary Theory and Criticism, British Fiction, South Asian Fiction, Diaspora Literature, and Romanticism.

Translator's Note

I got this collection of short stories from Dr Rattan Lal Talashi, former Professor, Dept. of Kashmiri, University of Kashmir. I got eager to render the stories into English after reading them. Prof. Talashi also encouraged me to translate them. I began to translate these short stories in the winter of 2017. And, slowly but surely, story after story was translated until I have reached the stage that all these stories, including the Afterword, are now in English.

The task of translating the Kashmiri short story is not easy. It is both exciting and challenging. More the latter than the former. The syntax of the original in this particular case is meandering, perhaps deliberately so, to convey the intricate emotions embedded in the experience of the Pandit community. So, no matter how much attempt is made, it is not going to work if a literal approach is adopted. The translator had to work his way into the kernel of the meaning conveyed and then to render the same into English. Then there are rituals and customs specific to the Kashmiri pandit community. It was important to understand and appreciate them so that translation occurred with a higher degree of faithfulness. Thirdly, there was a difficulty for the translator while reading the original because often the reported speech is not put in inverted commas. Very often making the distinction between two different voices was formidable because they seamlessly flow from one to the other without any mark of separation. To separate the speakers, and even the expression of inward thoughts, I have used inverted commas. That way it is easy for the reader to identify the speakers. Fourth, there is no consistent manner of inserting the 'pause' in the original, and there are so many of them. Wherever needed I have included an ellipsis, and sometimes a greater number of dots have been used to indicate a longer pause.

Most of these stories are about the Pandit experience in refugee camps of Jammu. The sense of Home is immanent, and there is a deep feeling of alienation from the surroundings in Jammu. The image of the cramped room is rife. In story after story, the reader is made to feel the space cramped for the migrated Kashmiri pandit. The room is emblematic of the cramped existence of the Kashmiri pandit away from his home in Kashmir. The community appears to be losing language, customs, and even members of the community, especially women, to other cultures and communities. The stories evoke a state of crisis both internal and external. The state of exile is a tragic inward condition. A large number of characters suffer from mental depression and are teetering on the edge of insanity, and language struggles to capture this experience.

There are twelve short stories in this collection. Ten of these short stories have been written after the migration of 1990. There are many examples of the pre-migration atmosphere and the warmth of characters and human relations which have got separated from their native soil and culture. These characters have the desire to guard those testimonies of mutual connectedness which were present before getting separated. There occurred a rupture but they are conscious of the belief that there was a connection. They are entrapped in politics but for them humanity is more important than politics. In exile how they have preserved their life and glory, and how the home was lost, this is the import of these stories.

This is not my first translation from Kashmiri to English. Earlier, I have also translated short stories and published them in journals. I am sure this will not be the last work in translation. I apologize for any error or mistake in this book. Any suggestion or advice with regard to this book, or translation in general, is more than welcome. I look forward to them.

1

Snow

(1979)

The age has brought its emptiness, a gift for each heart[1]
Good for them that they have yet preserved the warmth of traditions
With faith and same old belief, I bore the suffering
I am worried about your ailment, for whom are you?!

(Amin Kamil)

Abstract: *Divided into four parts under the sub-titles Srinagar, Bana Haal, Jammu, and Srinagar, the main focus of the story is the absence of snow in Kashmir for three years, and then its eventual fall at the end of the story.*

Mohan Lal and Mohi-ud-Din work in the same office. They return from Jammu after Mohi-ud-Din quarrels with the boss. Mohan Lal's daughter Babli, eagerly waiting for snow, asks him if snowfall has occurred on the Bana Haal mountain near the Jawahar Tunnel. After a day-long journey on the bus from Jammu, he is trying to sleep. In the section titled Bana Haal, he recalls the conversations in the bus about the fall of snow. Kashmir has not seen snowfall for the last three years. Finally, when Mohan Lal wakes up late in the day at his home in Kashmir, snow begins to fall, and there is joy all around.

SRINAGAR

A lot of time had passed yet sleep eluded Mohan Lal. He tried closing his eyes but found himself merely turning around in bed. Occasionally, he

---

[1] The year when this story was written.

Rupture. Rattan Lal Shant, Translated by Dr Javaid Iqbal Bhat, Oxford University Press. © Oxford University Press 2022. DOI: 10.1093/oso/9780192865083.003.0001

opened his eyes and with the help of the dim light passing through the newspaper pasted on the cracks, he wondered what time of the day it was? The glow passing through the paper was very faint. The bright light of the day did not manage to pass through. Even the little crevices of his room were covered with scraps of newspaper. He could only hear the breathing of his family members as if they were floating on the darkness and flailing their feet and arms. Mohan Lal was squirming in his bed.

He was feeling dizzy, and his head was reeling. Some strange dreamy images were filling his mind. He imagined that in the dim glow the room had shrunk and divided into small cages. Nothing else was visible. Sometimes, it seemed to him that these cages were magically spread out towards the edges; the corners of the room joining with the walls and the windowsill on the one side, and then doing the same on the other side. Sometimes these cages were sitting on top of one another in a stack and then getting stuck against each other in the emptiness of the sky.

He struck his forehead two or three times and turned to one side. He thought he had spotted the face of his wife in the dark. She had turned into a lifeless irregular ball of yarn in her bed in one corner of the room. Last night when they were up talking for a long time, she had told him, 'Go to sleep now. You must be tired.'

And she commanded Babli, 'Don't wake up your father until it is late enough so that he can get sound sleep.'

However, Mohan Lal did not sleep at all. His wife kept asking him about Jammu. Without really feeling anything, he kept replying 'yes' or 'no' to her questions. She figured out something naughty from his face and asked him.

'Get under the quilt now. You must be feeling crippled after travelling on this damned road from Jammu to Srinagar . . . sitting in one position in the bus from morning till evening!'

He was listening quietly. At the mention of the bus, his mind began to work, and he stared at his wife like a *Haanguil*.[2] His wife read his look and asked him with a smile. 'What did I tell you? Go to sleep now . . . Why are you looking at me in this manner? . . . You are tired and you must listen to me like a good boy.'

---

[2] Kashmiri word for a special breed of deer. It is found in the famous Dachigam National Park. It is an endangered species.

Mohan Lal understood the meaning his wife had derived from the way he was looking at her. He smiled and looked at her innocent behaviour with affection. After all, how could her manners change in just one month?

Then she got up from her position. She took off her *pheran*[3] and tried to put him to sleep against the pillow as if he were a child. She moved her fingers over his eyelids and tried to put him to sleep by comforting him in this way.

'Will tomorrow not come? Is everything over? Am I going anywhere? … Tonight you will feel like you are being rocked.' She consoled him.

She left and slipped under another quilt. She switched off the light and shouted across to him, 'Hope you won't tell me now that you are feeling cold. There is not much cold here in Kashmir. There is no snow yet. Even flurries haven't come yet. Looks like the weather in Jammu must be better than Srinagar.'

Actually, it was not cold, but he could not sleep even for a moment. Closing his eyes, he felt as if his bed was flying in space. He opened his eyes to see shadows floating and laughing out loud in the dim light.

BANA HAAL

As soon as Mohan Lal had entered home in the evening after a day-long journey from Jammu, Babli hugged him. After that, the first thing that Babli and his wife asked him was whether the snow had fallen on the Bana Haal[4] mountain. His wife knew that there was one very high peak at Bana Haal which stood between Jammu and Kashmir. From one side the bus went up and from the other side it came down and reached Jammu. If nowhere else at least over the Bana Haal mountain the snow must definitely be falling. Not for nothing does this road remain closed in winter, she used to think.

Mohan Lal continued to talk, and Babli felt strange hearing him. When she heard about the absence of snow on Bana Haal mountain, the joy of seeing her father after one month disappeared. Feeling sad, she left the lap

[3] A long woollen gown covering the body from the neck to below the knees, used to keep body warm during winter.

[4] A town, also known as the 'gateway of Kashmir', where the Jawahar Tunnel connects Jammu and Kashmir divisions of J&K.

of her father and began to look through the window. After some time, she got busy with the things outside. Her mother persuaded her to come back and asked her why she would not like to be with her father who had returned from Jammu after over a month. 'He must have got a lot of things for you.' But Babli was already lost in thought.

Mohan Lal placed her in his lap and started stroking her hair affectionately. 'Look, my dear! The snow might have fallen on the peaks of Bana Haal but now buses do not have to move up because they have made a hole in the mountain. The buses go through this big round hole and cross over to the other side.' So, I could not see the mountain peak for snowfall.

'Wow! Do buses manage to get inside the hole?' Babli began to show interest and Mohan Lal continued. 'Yes, they have made a big hole in the mountain. About the size of our home. It is called the Tunnel. There is a long road inside and the bus goes in from one side and comes out from the other.'

'Wow! Is there no suffocation inside the tunnel?'

'No. The air passes through the Tunnel. There are lights inside. But it did seem dark inside when we were in the bus and a child shrieked due to fright.... I will show you the Tunnel one day.' Mohan Lal said, recalling the scene inside the bus.

'No, I will never go through it.... I will be frightened inside.' Having said this Babli hid her head underneath his *pheran*. Mohan Lal felt perplexed and got lost in something. He began to think about the bus when it was moving towards Kashmir.

Earlier in the day when the bus had left the village of Bana Haal, and began to slowly go up the mountain, the light had appeared on the horizon. When the bus reached a curve, it swivelled like a top and in the cold, it made sounds as if it were a cold-afflicted horse. The passengers fell over each other and woke up from their naps. Mohan Lal was thrown over Mohi-ud-Din and sometimes Mohi-ud-Din was thrown over him. Mohan Lal's head was hung over his chest. Mohi-ud-Din woke up and lit a cigarette. He smoked to keep his mind awake. Someone on the back seat was also smoking and the rest of the passengers were napping or were seated quietly.

Mohi-ud-Din nudged Mohan Lal, 'Hey, your head will strike against something. Wake up.' Mohan Lal whispered something, rubbed his eyes, and placed his head on Mohi-ud-Din's shoulder. The bus went inside the Tunnel. A child in the bus had suddenly issued out a shout, cracking through the silence.

'The poor fellow must have been frightened by the dark. Hey Sardarji! Please switch on the lights,' one of the passengers requested the driver.[5]

'No, he won't switch on the lights. Why should he waste the government battery?!' a young man threw out this joking remark.

'Yes, did you not see since morning, by putting the bus into neutral gear repeatedly, he has bored us. Perhaps he wants to make sure that we reach home late at night,' the first one replied.

'Yes, that is right. He must save petrol and then sell it in the market for his pocket.'

The conversation stretched from the corruption of the driver to the thievery of the government officials, to faithless people, and then of course to India and Pakistan.

There was a heated discussion. Mohi-ud-Din gave Mohan Lal a cigarette. 'Have it, your sleep will disappear. Listen to the discussion. You might have become bored in the silence.'

Mohan Lal lit the cigarette and turned to Mohi-ud-Din. 'No one on the bus is now telling the Sardarji about putting on the lights. They've forgotten that.'

This might have been heard by the young man sitting at the back. He could not bear it and turned to Mohan Lal, 'Sir, why this taunting? *You* should have told him that.' The other young man also could not bear it all and he shouted at the driver, 'Sardarji, Sardarji, stop the vehicle!'

The driver hit the brakes and the vehicle came to a jerky halt. The passengers knocked against the windows and the railings. The driver was angry and amazed. Mohi-ud-Din spoke to the young man, 'Is this the way to shout at the driver? He must have been frightened. See how he applied the brakes. Thank God, we are still inside the tunnel. Had we been on the open road, an accident would have happened.'

The young man retorted, 'You please remain quiet and mind your business. I shouted at the driver, why are you in distress?'

Mohi-ud-Din got up, ready to quarrel. However, Mohan Lal caught hold of him and covered his mouth shut. Yet the driver knew nothing

---

[5] Sardarji is a respectful way of addressing a Sikh.

about this row in the darkness. He switched on the light and asked them, 'What is the matter, Mister? Why did you ask me to stop the bus?'

The father of the scared child replied, 'Now that you have switched on the light, you can move on. The child is afraid of the dark that is why we were asking.'

The driver turned to the young man, 'For such a small thing, why were you getting angry? You should have told me, and I would have switched on the light!'

'We have been saying that ever since we entered the tunnel. Did you not hear the shriek of my child?' 'I swear by the Guru I did not hear it. This is the problem with the first gear. It begins to sob, making the *wuu wuu* sound. Like an old wife.' And he shouted at the conductor of the bus, 'Hey, Fauja Singha! Where the hell are you?! Are you dead?!'

'Let us move on now. God knows what time it is! It will be so kind of you if we can reach home earlier,' said the father of the scared child.

The bus left and the second young man turned to the scared child's father with reproach,

'Why did you seem like you were begging him? Stubborn driver! I will see to it that he drives us to home earlier!!!'

But the father had taken the child from the mother's lap into his own. His wife vomited from underneath her *burka* into a glass and then threw it out of the window. She was looking pale and haggard due to vomiting and dizziness the whole day. Occasionally she felt fidgety and her husband fanned her with cardboard. Sometimes she felt cold and he would wrap her in a *chaddar*.[6] Several times she felt like vomiting and her husband held the glass under the burka. When this happened Mohan Lal and Mohi-ud-Din held their son.

It seemed the young man was not yet content. He turned to Mohan Lal, 'You shouldn't feel upset. I deliberately reproached the driver.'

Mohan Lal and Mohi-ud-Din looked at each other. The young one was saying, 'They should be feeling disappointed after crossing Bana Haal into Kashmir. They act like lions when they are on the Jammu side of the tunnel. They do not listen to us.'

---

[6] A coarse woollen cloth traditionally woven from wool and used by old people, especially in winter.

The other young man turned to Mohi-ud-Din, 'Did you notice how the Sikh is now speaking in Kashmiri? During the day he spoke only in Punjabi!'

'All their vanity goes away after crossing Bana Haal,' the first young man said.

Mohi-ud-Din looked at Mohan Lal. There was a restlessness in his eyes because he was trying his best to calm himself down.

The mouth of the Tunnel came into view. Two labourers seated behind laid a bet. One of them said that snow must have fallen in Kashmir and the other said that only yesterday a labourer had come from Kashmir and told that there was no snow.

For three years, there had been no snow. Just dry weather.

People used to talk about it in homes, markets, and fields, wherever someone mentioned snow. The attention of the passengers also turned towards snow. All the passengers must have been pining for snow across the Jammu side of the Tunnel.

Mohi-ud-Din spoke as if talking to himself, 'What is the snowfall going to give you—a treasure? You are breaking each other's heads for nothing!!!'

Mohan Lal cast a surprised look at him and saw him looking bitter and sucking at the fag end of the cigarette held between his fingers.

'A good snowfall means a good harvest of rice. In the past people used to be looking at the sky for snow from autumn onwards.'

A smile appeared on Mohan Lal's face. He turned towards Mohi-ud-Din,

'Yes, Mohda.[7] Does not rice grow with snow now? Does that not require water? What is the other source of water for us other than the snow-covered mountains? What is the other source of water for our crops?'

Mohi-ud-Din bit his lip under his teeth. 'Okay! For our crops! It does not matter to me whether they sow seeds or not! What difference will it make? In either situation, we have to take the rice from Punjab!'

Then he began to stare at the mouth of the Tunnel. As it got nearer a twittering noise grew inside the bus. He told Mohan Lal without looking at him, 'I do not become emotional when I see snow.'

---

[7] Informal for Mohi-ud-Din.

A wave of life seemed to exude from the windows of the bus as it crossed the Tunnel into Kashmir. The windows opened with a clatter, and the passengers began to see snow on the mountain peaks through the darkness. Right then the driver spoke to the passengers in a loud voice, 'O! Forget about the snow! Kashmir has become like Punjab now.' And with that, he put the bus into neutral mode down the slope.

The young man sensed an opportunity, and he told Mohan Lal,

'Did you see, sir? What he spat out of his mouth! He's saying that Kashmir is turning into Punjab.'

The other one chipped in, 'With two butts of the head I would have broken all his teeth.' He began to shake his head like an injured snake.

'He's back in his chattering groove,' the first young man broke in.

This time Mohi-ud-Din did not wait for Mohan Lal. He got up and scolded both youngsters, 'Enough of your mindless chatter! He did not lie! Has it not become worse than Punjab in Kashmir? It has been three years without snow!'

'Last winter we did not even see rain,' a passenger seconded Mohi-ud-Din's statement.

The young men fell silent. Mohi-ud-Din continued with his talk, 'And what fortune are you going to get from the snow? Please tell me that?'

'Whether or not we get a fortune is our headache. Why is he in pain? Why does he bother so much?!' one of the men told Mohi-ud-Din making him understand the point.

The other one explained, 'Look, everything on the other side of the mountain is theirs. Don't you see what a flowery, energetic self they present when they are in Jammu ... ? Moreover, he has to drive the bus. He is telling us that Kashmir should each year become like Punjab.' Then he stared at Mohan Lal as if daring him to say something in response.

'Only the Kashmiri farmer knows! Each one of the poor Kashmiri farmers!' said the young man. He drew a *Karakuili*[8] cap and a *duissa*[9] from his bag, put on the cap, and threw the *duissa* around himself. Mohan Lal was looking through the window. He felt like lost in the darkness and remembered the sense of vivacity he had felt in Jammu during the last month.

---

[8] A karakuil hat is a hat made from the karakuil breed of sheep.
[9] A shawl used by Kashmiri men and women.

The child-carrying father looked behind. He was fed up with throwing away his wife's vomit.

The youngster read support in this backward glance of the man and spoke philosophically, 'Our blood and flesh are made of this snow.'

The father did not respond to this innuendo. His child had woken up because of the talk going on in the bus, and he was trying to lull him to sleep.

Mohi-ud-Din nudged Mohan Lal, and passed a cigarette to him, 'What are you looking at on that side in the darkness? Hold this and smoke! There is no point paying attention to these young men.'

After that, the youngsters fell silent and the bus continued to move on.

JAMMU

Mohi-ud-Din and Mohan Lal had to stay for some more time in Jammu, but ever since Mohi-ud-Din had quarrelled with the boss, they kept their belongings ready, expecting their boss to kick them back to Srinagar any day.

The year was drawing to its end, and like any 'patriot' the Engineer Sahab was worried about how to spend the unutilized funds. That is why he decided to meet the Minister in Jammu and get the works allotted to the contractors. The cooperation of the Accountant Mohi-ud-Din was necessary in this process. The clerk Mohan Lal was Mohi-ud-Din's buddy. Mohi-ud-Din had contrived for Mohan Lal to accompany him to Jammu. Mohan Lal took it as an opportunity to see Jammu. When Mohi-ud-Din quarrelled with the boss, Mohan Lal also received orders to return from Jammu.

Initially, Mohan Lal did not like Jammu but that changed later. Mohi-ud-Din showed him each market and mohalla like a professional guide. Jammu was not even as big as *Raenwor*,[10] not to talk of Srinagar. And Mohan Lal would carelessly wander about the places like a solitary man, a person without any family.

After leaving their office, Mohan Lal and Mohi-ud-Din used to stroll through Raghunath Market a number of times without any stop.

[10] A neighbourhood in Srinagar.

Mohi-ud-Din met many of his friends. At first, they would greet him with a 'salaam' but after meeting him twice or thrice, they would just pass by, sometimes with a smile. Mohan Lal did not meet a single acquaintance. Mohi-ud-Din was wondering whether Mohan Lal had any relatives at all in Jammu. He did not have any relatives in Jammu. His parents were also not alive so that he could trace connections with relatives with their help. They lived in rented accommodation with a friend, who was also without his family, and came to Jammu with the *Darbar Move*.[11]

Mohi-ud-Din told Mohan Lal that the streets of Jammu are similar. You should prefer to walk a little more on the main roads than taking the alleys and streets, he advised him. One could get lost in the narrow streets. Mohan Lal used to lose his way every day but it did not bother him. He saw concrete buildings and schools in marketplaces. After every step there was a tea shop. And when he noticed any woman with a *chaddhar* and wearing a *pheran*, he desired to speak to her in Kashmiri. And when he saw women on the flat roofs enjoying the sunlight, drying their hair and busy with washing utensils or clothes, he would pray for them in his mind like an elder. He promised himself that he would take his children and wife to Jammu the next year. The boss was kind, and he could avail three more months for a holiday.

But Mohi-ud-Din had quarrelled with the boss, and now all of this was impossible! He sighed.

On Eid they were in Jammu and Mohan Lal told Mohi-ud-Din, 'Listen, let us go and say Eid Mubarak to the boss. It is better to keep good relations.'

Mohi-ud-Din replied, 'Forget about it. It is pointless and counterproductive. The untouchable of this place is better than him. I hate all!!'

'Now, we should not let it weigh on your mind! Afterall, he is one of our own. He is our officer,' Mohan Lal tried to reason with him.

'That is the problem. He shows his real nature only to his own. He cannot dare show it to anyone!!'

Mohan Lal felt something contorting in his inner self.

Days passed and Mohi-ud-Din's spite towards their boss kept increasing.

---

[11] The movement of the Government offices from Srinagar (the summer capital) to Jammu (the winter capital) and vice versa.

Mohan Lal was missing his family back in Kashmir. He tried to tell himself, 'Forget about Mohi-ud-Din. He is a vagrant—whether he is in Jammu or Kashmir.' When Mohan Lal roamed around in Jammu, he was reminded of the children clinging to the *Kaengdis*[12] in Kashmir for keeping warm. 'The frostbite must have turned their hands and feet fat like big earthen pots. And if snow has fallen in Kashmir, there will be the charm after a long time,' he thought. 'The children do need the snowbird[13] to play with. Who will make the snowman for them? The straps are to be fixed on the *khraav*.[14] But next year I will definitely bring them here. The children will have fun and rollick about in warm weather. My wife will also blossom like the women who come to Jammu with the *Darbar Move*.'

Mohi-ud-Din was still in the grip of anger and told Mohan Lal, 'Does the boss think I will return to Kashmir? He is dreaming. I will stay back until March. He will explode open if he consumes the ill-gotten money all by himself.'

Eventually, both Mohan Lal and Mohi-ud-Din had to return to Kashmir. Mohan Lal took it as a good prospect but Mohi-ud-Din was crushed.

SRINAGAR

Mohan Lal's wife told him that he would feel the jerks and pull off his bus journey in his body the whole night. Once in her childhood she had been to Dal Lake in a boat along with her family. Then she had felt in a vortex the whole night.

He could not get any rest or sleep. He was just turning in his bed the whole night. Once when he dozed off, he saw himself in the warmth of Jammu and the children swollen with cold in Kashmir. He saw himself trapped in the tunnel, with darkness in front and behind. On both sides he saw people holding blazing sticks. He jumped from the mountains and was thrown into the forests and the fields. But people dug him out.

---

[12] The conventional firepot used by Kashmiris to keep themselves warm during the cold season. It is filled with charcoal.

[13] The original word is *Paetchin Puut*, a bird caught in winter season with a snare.

[14] A type of winter shoegear not used these days. It has a thick heavy wood sole and the straps are made of straws and dried grass.

He woke up in the afternoon. Babli was singing by the window and clapping. 'Snowfall, come! Come!'

There may have been a number of children in the courtyard. The noise of their rollicking and playing was in the air. Then his wife came and reprimanded Babli, 'Did I not tell you not to wake him up? He slept late in the night. Go down to the courtyard and play in the snow with the children.'

'Has snow fallen?' Mohan Lal lifted his head from the pillow.

It seemed the face of his wife was a glowing crimson. She was happy.

'It has been falling for quite a while. Get up and see through the window. Looks like the plants and trees have worn whites.' She seemed ecstatic and went outside.

Mohan Lal sat up in bed and rubbed his eyes. He could not believe his eyes when he saw big flakes of snow falling from the roof. He lit a cigarette. His wife came with a plate. She told him to have some *Taehar*, which she had cooked for distribution among people, especially children.[15]

'*Taehar?*' He was surprised and began to scan his wife's face.

'Today snow fell after three years. We were pining for the snow. Our hearts had become hopeless. Babli, come here and give a little of this rice to the children of Pinki and Bitta.'

Mohan Lal took some rice but he was looking at his wife as if bewildered.

'What are you looking at? Get up and wash your hands and face. Come, let us go to Deena Habb Sahab's[16] place and untie the thread because the prayer for snow has been answered.'

---

[15] Rice cooked with turmeric, hence yellow. The practice of distributing this rice among passers-by continues.

[16] Name of a shrine.

2

The Hunter

(1981)

Abstract: *The narrator's wife is musing by the side of the window. She is watching a crane in the Dal Lake. Her husband's hunter friend has come to catch the crane. Her husband is asking for the key of the storeroom so that he can take the logs and make a boat for his friend. She is unhappy that her husband is arranging a boat for the hunter. Later some boys arrange the boat, and the hunter is going to catch the beautiful crane. The husband assures her that the crane will not be killed. The wife seems to identify herself with the condition of the crane, with memories of how her house in Kashmir was pounded with stones by neighbourhood boys (probably Muslims).*

'Have you ever pondered over it? Doesn't this mountain, clad in a self-coloured *duissa* and a turban of sunshine, appear to have seated for some serious talk.' She sat beside a window on a sunny day of Autumn. She appeared to be carrying something by dint of her looks to the summit of the mountain across the lake. When she saw me standing beside her, she said to me again, 'Doesn't it look as if the *Jogis*[1] by the foot of the mountain have hung their saffron coloured clothes on the twigs of willows and chinars?'

'These are nothing but the changing colours of autumn. You seem to have become a poet. But what have you thought about me?' I asked her.

She did not appear to be in the mood for any light talk. She blushed. The circles around her eyes had disappeared. The irises had sunk and become narrow. The glow on her face was such that I had witnessed never before. For a little while, I felt that the memories of thousands of years and experiences of old books had spread around her like a circle of light. That

---

[1] These are ascetic people, followers of yoga. They wear saffron-coloured clothes.

Rupture. Rattan Lal Shant, Translated by Dr Javaid Iqbal Bhat, Oxford University Press. © Oxford University Press 2022. DOI: 10.1093/oso/9780192865083.003.0002

aura was in the midst of this window, and she was standing in its centre. I felt stunned and kept looking at her. Without looking at me, she said,

'Behold! How the raw sky seems to be getting peace by wrapping its restless senile form in the clean, mirror-like water of the lake. Did you ever ponder from where this lone crane came to the lake? It is always measuring its strides amid *Pandchan* and *Neeljan*.[2] God knows from which herd this poor bird has been separated?! What pure white wings, long neck, and long lanky legs it has! How many days has it been wandering on this island on the Dal Lake from one place to another? Neither can it fly away nor, like *Neeljan*, take a dip in the lake.'

Standing behind her, I was in a fix. Shall I take her out from this dream-like state or let her, for some time, elucidate this state of dreams or ideas? But then I was dismayed by her question.

'What is crane called in Kashmiri? Have you ever seen such a big crane in the Delhi zoo?'

'No,' I spoke the truth. 'God knows whether cranes are found in Kashmir or not?' Perhaps there are. I have seen birds like vultures in the sanctuary of Dachigam making nests high in the trees and feeding small fishes to their young ones. But this strange bird in the lake in front of my house roused none of my interest except urging me to think that it might be a crane. I did not expect that this naïve woman would think so much over this bird and raise such questions. A crane in a lake, a mountain behind the lake, and the sky over the mountain—that was all I could see from the window. But she saw so much more than I could see.

'God knows whether it finds a mention in old Kashmiri Sanskrit books,' she posed this question as if to herself. Now I had an apprehension of getting myself lost in the many generations of birds. So, at once, I returned to my point, 'Give me the key of the storeroom. Had we not kept the logs there on the floor?'

It was quite plain that she did not hear me. After a while she remarked, 'This crane should have been reared in some sanctuary here! Isn't it good that it could reach here? Not sure, whether it has come from Siberia or is an old species of some Kashmiri bird ... ?'

I too thought that it was like a water-vulture, but its beak was a little straighter. It looked like a sky swan of some folktale. But holding tight

---

[2] Two types of birds.

to the patch of land it seemed to have found a resting place after a long time. I forgot about the storeroom in which besides logs we had put some earthenwares.

'What is the point of rearing it here? Useless burden ... ! There are hundreds in Delhi,' I told her as if I was being asked to rear it.

She was filled with enthusiasm like a child. I went away silently and entered the kitchen.

She used to keep the bunch of keys somewhere on the windowsill. I touched something accidentally and the utensils fell with a clang. She came over quickly saying some insane things.

'Did you enter again with your boots on? What have you laid your dirty dog-like hands on?' She was gripping her head while sitting down confused and remorseful as if languidly coming out of a dream. Oh! How she got up a little and handed me the bunch of keys! I immediately realized that in having jolted her from the world of cranes in Sanskrit books and the company of Jogi brothers into the disordered room of utensils, I had committed a mistake. On any other day, she would have searchingly asked me what I was doing in her empire. That is why I told her myself, the hunter has come to catch the crane. "Today he does not have to kill .... but says he will trap the crane alive and then sell it to some zoo."

Hearing this, her face began to flame again and her earlobes turned red like the autumn chinar leaves and the rage spread to all parts of her body. That is why I told her,

'See! Whether this crane has come from distant Siberia or Central Asia or the cliffs of the Himalayas or the old species of Kashmiri birds or be it a new bird, the reality is that this time it is stuck helplessly in the lake. It will be killed by some hunter sooner or later. Would it not be better that this hunter catches it alive and takes it for rearing ... ? I told him I would make a boat of logs and then set sail on that.'

'You will make a boat for him? Can't he do it himself? Why are you showing him sympathy?' she said pithily.

'He is my friend after all. It is perchance that our house stands on the bank of this lake. Now if he came to our home for it, should I drive him away?'

'When did I tell you to drive him away? If he is your friend, ask him why his son joined in pelting our house with stones on the day of the cricket match?'

She still remembered the day when their house was pounded with stones. 'If that neighbour, the old *Haji*³ had not come in the way, the boys would have demolished our home. What a great personality was that snow-white-bearded Haji whose luminous and glowing face had prompted my American black friend to yell, "Oh Moses!" He still writes from America. Though feeling remorse for being a black (in white America), he asks unfailingly "Moses is alive?"'

I replied, 'He is alive and his followers as well.' But I haven't till date been able to understand whether our relations are religious in nature or a form of compromise in an adverse situation. I feel nostalgic about coming across that *Haji* because I think that his generation is on the wane. I don't know why *Haji*, too, heaves a sigh of relief on meeting me.

'What had happened was now part of the past. It is unwise to open the wound again,' replied my wife without much thought. I returned from the desert of imagination and went down with a bunch of keys. She quickly came down after me. The hunter was there cleaning the barrel of the gun with the help of a rope, passing it through, and oiling it. The entire house smelt of oil.

I began to move the utensils in the room. The logs lay underneath the things and it was not easy to bring them out. She would have been watching it.

'I have piled up things of so many years there—boxes over boxes. Things of marriage functions, vases of flowers, earthen pots used during the *havvan*⁴ to pour dry fruits over the fire. You will break them all! You will throw in disarray or ruin all the things. It is so because the hunter is your friend and you have to build a boat for him so that he catches the crane. Oh God! Oh God!' She said in despair.

Again, she could not but sit down. Again, the old colour of autumn smeared her face. I fetched water and offered her to drink it, sprinkled her face with water. With great difficulty she said, 'Do what you have to. Why would you worry about me? This disease of despair and fear of losing things will return to me every spring and autumn for one reason or the other. Today this crane came like the god of death.'

---

³ A Muslim who has performed the Hajj. Generally used for old, bearded men.
⁴ Havana or Havvan means the act of offering oblations in the fire.

My arms and legs, too, failed me. How I will enter the room and what would I tell my hunter friend? I thought I would tell him I was mistaken and the logs were fastened to the floor.

Then a miracle happened. A miracle because I was cleared of the obligation effortlessly. My hunter friend came to me, 'Oh! Take it easy. I got the boat arranged. Thank you!'

I ran in to inform her. She was rearranging things in the storeroom. She spoke to me, 'What kind of friend he is after all! You don't dare to ask him even about petty things. Okay, don't ask him. You cannot do anything. But don't you feel a bit? Has he to do this bloodbath only here at my house? How do you tolerate it? Poor crane!'

I was dumbfounded. I could not speak to her; nor was I able to ask the hunter anything. I was wondering whether the hunter had read my face. Because he said, 'Don't worry, the gunshot will be fired just to frighten the crane. Actually, I have to ensnare it in this net.'

He was tying pieces of auburn cloth to adjust the mesh of the net.

We heard a conversation going on outside and came out. There we found some boys bringing down a small boat from a jeep. He shouted to me with a ring of pride, 'Do you see what we grown-ups cannot do, these youth can do so well.'

Holding my wife's arm, I went inside with her lest she spotted the hunter's son in the group of these boys.

'You are all alike .... You are no different from this friend of yours. All alike! All!' She said. I shut the windows tight.

3

Separation

(1994)

Abstract: *This is a post-migration story. A story of the loss of Roshan Lal's mother Arni, Kashmir, and Roshan's niece, Usha. The latter gets married outside the community against the wishes of Roshan Lal. The main character Roshan Lal is living with some other Kashmiri pandits in a tent in a refugee colony in Jammu. Roshan Lal's mother has died a few days ago. He appears to be lost in sadness. When his niece Usha comes to visit him along with her husband Ajeet Kumar, Roshan is still in the same state, and people are trying to bring him out of despondency. Towards the end, people feel glad when he gets up to speak, but he only ends up talking about his father who has died twenty years ago in Kashmir!*

Roshan Lal sat quietly as if dumb. He neither spoke nor was answering anyone. People came to meet and sat wherever they could find a place to sit. And when they sat down, they asked people on their right and left, 'Has Roshan Lal returned to the normal state?'

The person who answered this question shook his head and pushed his lips forward as if saying, 'I don't think so. Still, who knows....? Maybe he will come back to normal condition!' The questioner would look towards Roshan Lal who wore a *pheran*, deploring himself with his downcast head. Even if he was forced to answer, he would just make some inane noises and again drop his head down. The questioner would soon forget about the mourning of Roshan and participate in some social or political discussion, which used to go on there the whole day.

Today, on the seventh day also, some relatives appeared for the consolation of Roshan Lal. Almost all of his relatives had already come. Then Roshan Lal's niece, Usha, and her husband Ajeet Kumar stood in front of the tent for males and the discussion stopped and all looked towards

Rupture. Rattan Lal Shant, Translated by Dr Javaid Iqbal Bhat, Oxford University Press. © Oxford University Press 2022. DOI: 10.1093/oso/9780192865083.003.0003

them. Usha was wiping her tears with her handkerchief. Ajeet Kumar was wearing jeans pant and a T-shirt. Usha was looking towards Roshan Lal, who had cast his head down, and it seemed she did not know anyone else. In the silence, it seemed as if poor Ajeet Kumar had been caught stealing. He did not know whether he should leave or go inside. He put his attaché down and began to look sheepishly at his wife, as if telling her, 'This is your maternal home. Only you can help me out here.'

Right then Badri Nath, affectionately called Bodh *Maam*,[1] popped up from somewhere. He took hold of Ajeet Kumar's hand and took him inside the tent. He respectfully created some space near Roshan Lal and asked him to sit there. Then he told him, 'Death evens out the ground.... Death is a great leveller.... Sit down, everything will be alright. There is no need to feel worried.'

The onlookers were trying to find on Ajeet Kumar's face a line that could be read as that of sorrow or mourning. They did not see anything.

Usha continued to weep, and then Bodh *Maam* went near her, and took hold of her hand and brought her in the direction of the tent reserved for the females. He jumped over the ropes and stumps holding the tent, leapt over the little water outlets; however, Usha appeared to be inexperienced in doing this despite being a village girl.

The discussion which had stopped due to the arrival of the guest restarted in whispers.

It seemed Ajeet Kumar was itching to explain their delayed arrival but he was still shy enough to speak. He tried to look towards Roshan Lal but it was of no avail because Roshan sat with his head cast down all the time. Ajeet Kumar bided his time counting the straws of the mat or, while keeping his eyes focused downwards, inwardly observing the people who were seated on the mat. He was waiting for Bodh *Maam* so that he could talk with him.

Bodh *Maam* was carrying Usha over the ropes to the tent meant for female mourners. 'Come this way and jump! Jump! Don't be afraid. This ground here is all uneven. But it will be even. It will be leveled by itself.' He was telling Usha.

Controlling her tears and holding the hand of Bodh *Maam*, Usha was moving hastily and counting her leaps. When a sleeve of her trouser was

[1] Uncle; usually the brother of one's mother.

caught in a stump, she fell on her face. Or perhaps Bodh *Maam* pulled her hand and she fell. Like a football, she fell on a rope and after turning around rolled down. The slope went down all the way to the rivulet where there were hot boulders in place of water. Thousands of round boulders. She did not know whether it was because of Bodh *Maam* or herself that she had slipped. Both of them went rolling down.

All the men got out of the tent and ran towards the slope. All this could be seen from the other tent. When on this seventh day their eyes had caught sight of the Usha, silence had descended on the whole tent. The accident saved her from hearing the taunts of the women. The taunts like, 'Now, on the seventh day arrived the grandmothers for weeping!' She was thinking that the cold welcome that she had received meant she would have to wail a little louder in front of the women.

But as soon as she fell, her maternal and paternal aunts came to her and lifted her. One started kneading her back and the other pressed her legs. One of them brought lemonade for her. Her feet started cramping. To enable her to walk, her husband lifted her in an embrace. And in this way, they brought her to a seating place. All of them came back to their respective positions.

Once Roshan Lal raised his eyes, and as soon as Usha walked a step, he dropped down his head.

The conversation resumed among people;

'God saved her. Otherwise, the rivulet might have also turned red.'

'First of all, why did she have to go with Bodh *Maam*? It made little difference to him.'

'Well, it is the fate of us all Kashmiri Hindus. She might have been living in some bungalow. She got trapped in our bad luck.'

'How did she know that her grandmother had passed away? Now she might have heard. Here no one even spoke to her!'

Right then Bodh *Maam* came limping and went to Roshan Lal. Sitting in front of him, Bodh *Maam* started growling at him in a loud voice, 'I told you I will seek an apology. Why don't you tell Arni? ... Remember, you will regret! Arni is dead! Long live Arni! Long live!' With a quick shrug, he went out. He had a cutting of an Urdu newspaper in his hand, and he hurled it towards Ajeet Kumar. He tried to see what had been published but not being able to read Urdu he dropped it and passed it to the next person who read it and passed it on to the next person. They took turns to read the cutting. There was silence all around. Bodh *Maam* was not saying anything wrong. Poor Ajeet Kumar felt as if his wings had been broken as he looked at their faces. He was wondering what was written in the newspaper. Finally, one of the men told him in a low voice, 'Someone has said in Kashmir that if Hindu migrants apologise, they can return to Kashmir.'

This fell flat on Ajeet Kumar. He was at a loss to understand the matter. It seemed to him that the mourners were talking in some coded language, only understood by them.

'Which organization has said it? Why?' he asked.

The person who read the news item regretted that he had told this to a stranger. How much shall I make him understand? He broke the reference to this matter. The people, who had been talking freely about political issues, suddenly turned into scared kittens and were gripped by their respective anxieties. They began to search for Bodh *Maam* all around, hoping he might show them some way out.

Amid all this, emerged the voice of Roshan Lal, recalling the words of his mother.

'She told me to bring snow for her feet. She wished to extinguish the fire of her soles. I had got a little snow with Pinta's help in the morning. That was used for water.' With these words, he stared behind the tents at the rain-filled rivulet, which was packed with boulders.

Roshan Lal's voice startled the people, some were both bewildered and happy that he at least spoke something. But Roshan Lal did not continue. When everybody lost hope of his return to conversation and were certain that he had descended into the ocean of silence again, Roshan Lal picked up a strand, 'In blistering heat, I went up to the city. How could I get snow in Jammu! Like a child, she went after me insisting to take her to *Shah Koal*.[2] I couldn't help it. I took her on the bicycle carrier to the bank of the canal. Sitting on the bank and putting her feet in the water, she asked me with great affection, 'Now that we have reached here, it won't take a long time before we reach there. Take me there on the bicycle, over this bank of the canal. She said that she wished to take a bath in the holy Mattan spring in Kashmir.'[3]

---

[2] Name of a canal in South Kashmir. It was constructed by the 14th-century king Bud Shah.
[3] The famous spring near the Martand temple in South Kashmir.

Roshan Lal again went into deep contemplation and began to sob. 'Nagabal Mattan. ... Nagabal Mattan.' He repeated this expression while shaking his head as if in meditation. He recalled the names of the sacred places of Hindus in Kashmir!

It was known to all that he did not leave any of his mother's wishes unfulfilled. Arni, Roshan Lal's mother, was much loved and respected in the tent refugee colony. Doing an errand for her was considered fortunate by the residents, and the whole colony was like a courtyard to her. Otherwise, what was common between the refugees of south and north Kashmir? It was Arni who was bringing them close to each other for support. When a wind started to blow, she would pick up Roshan Lal and Pinto and come out, alerting the refugees;

'Are you there inside Moti Lal! There sitting next to your mother and taking apart the clean strands of wool?! This is not your stormy Kashmir wind that will spare you because you are a Kashmiri. It will take you wrapped in that tent and deposit you in the fire.' She hit down the stumps and tightened the ropes of the tent while saying these things. During the monsoon, the rain used to pour through the tattered tents and again Arni used to come out to do something, 'Hey Janki Nath, instead of making arrangement to collect rainwater in a plate or utensil you had better deepen the outlet around the tent.'

The death of Arni had been deeply felt by all the people in the colony but now more than that this expression of sorrow and worry on Roshan Lal's face was breaking their hearts.

One old man got up inside the tent, 'Hey, will you please listen to me? I am today on the seventh day of Arni's death in this tent, in broad daylight, with full control over my senses ... I ... I.' He stammered.

On the right side, someone tugged at his shirt, 'Hey, please sit down ... making sounds of "ba ba" like that of an old goat ... somehow Roshan had opened his mouth to speak and you are up like a pole.... Please sit down.' But the old man did not sit down, 'If you tell me I can give you in writing on an affidavit that this person who will come to see us from Delhi and then give his report to the Prime Minister ... the one who will see with his own eyes ... the one who will come with his own eyes ... tell him ... from my side, for I don't know if I will be alive until then or not.'

Now they began to tease him, 'Hey, your age is very long.... You will be here only with us.... Because if you are not here, who will roll up our tents when we go to Kashmir. Even after we leave, you will have to guard these tents because maybe we have to come back again.'

But the old man did not stop talking. He completed his announcement sitting down and opening his hands for prayer, 'May he return safe and sound! May God guard his light and give him strength. May he rise from progress to progress! May he only fly by airplanes! Rest in government guest houses! May he receive both TA and DA! And go on tours. We will serve him in life. He is with the wishes of the dead. They are innocent! They died for no fault of theirs. This is there for him.... Their prayer.'

He swooned and only after being given some water returned to consciousness. Then he sat up to wipe his tears.

Like Narad, Bodh *Maam* appeared from nowhere and told them, 'Dears, the old man might have got a letter.' Then he went to Ajeet Kumar and told him, 'You also look into the envelope and try to figure out the meaning.' And he went out with a smile on his face.

Ajeet Kumar asked someone what the letter was all about. He had sensed that Bodh *Maam*'s insinuation was meaningful. He was made to understand that the old man's son was a bank clerk in Kashmir. His son was one day killed as he had left his home. Ajeet responded, 'But why was he killed? Tell me the whole story.'

The person did not tell him because Roshan Lal had again raised his head.

'I am wondering what happened to his capacity to think. That is what is distressing me,' the person said. Roshan's eyes were brimming with tears—for the first time in the last seven days.

On the day Arni died, he did not have to do anything. The news of her death spread very fast in the entire colony. Everyone was shocked, and all of them gathered in front of Roshan Lal's tent. Arni was taken to the ghat like a flower. Roshan Lal looked like a wedding host who had left with the wedding party.

Two days before her death she called me and told me confidentially, 'Hold consultation with your brothers and construct another storey.' She told me that she had spoken to Aasha, Rani, and Chuuna. 'They will go to their maternal home along with their children in a fortnight.' She told me not to be like Bodh *Maam*, and start constructing separate homes. 'Make another storey of this very house. There is a treasure of seven generations in the walls of this house.' I learned that very moment that her death is imminent. I called Aasha and told her, 'you are lucky to be here with your mother for some time.'

When he talked about his mother, it seemed Roshan Lal saw her before his eyes.

Ajeet Kumar thought that the time was appropriate. He had not understood anything but when he saw tears in Roshan Lal's eyes, he saw that he was talking about his mother. Meanwhile, someone signalled to him to speak to Roshan Lal expecting the latter might talk. The people around urged him to ask him about his home in Kashmir. Ajeet Kumar asked him, 'Dear uncle! I have heard that your home in Kashmir is located at a beautiful place.'

Roshan Lal was so outraged. The person who had prodded Ajeet Kumar to speak was scared that Roshan Lal would hit him. Ajeet knew that Roshan Lal was against Usha's marriage with him. After the death of his younger sister, Sarwa, Roshan had brought up and educated Usha. After coming to Jammu, some relative of his brother-in-law brought Ajeet Kumar's marriage proposal for Usha. Roshan Lal opposed the match but Usha's father and uncle and aunts on the paternal side supported it. They said that she would go to the village home in Jammu and take some respite, this girl without a mother! The boy was from a zamindar family of Basoli besides doing a good business in Jammu. What if they are not Kashmiris?

However, Roshan Lal thought that Usha would be cut off from her family. And that proved to be true. With each passing day, the distance between her and her relatives increased. She lost her company and companions. She lost her native Kashmiri language. She came back there after six years and that too on the death of her grandmother. Roshan Lal stayed away from Usha's wedding, and now that old disgust returned to his eyes.

His brother Badri Nath (Bodh *Maam*) had interceded saying that it was predestined for her. Roshan Lal had told him, 'Maybe so! But I do not accept that.' Roshan Lal did not know that destiny would play sport with him, his mother, Bodh *Maam* and the rest of them. Who could have thought they would be torn away from Kashmir like limbs from a body? The flood of circumstances washed away the land of Khanabal and the border of Khadanyar.[4] How could they be fine in Jammu in the body or soul or language?

---

[4] The two geographical extremes in Kashmir.

Roshan Lal was gazing at Ajeet Kumar as if he was trying to recognize him. The young man fathomed courage and asked him, 'I pine to see your village and your home in Kashmir. Now the condition is good there. Yesterday, I had gone to my village in Basoli. My mother and father were saying that a man had returned from Kashmir hale and hearty after five days.'

Roshan Lal got up at once.

The people around him, his friends and relatives, could not believe their eyes. Slowly, Roshan Lal came out. All the people started congratulating Ajeet Kumar for bringing Roshan Lal out from a state of utter sorrow.

Meanwhile, Bodh *Maam* came running.

'Roshan Lal have you heard . . . ? Don't tell me later that you don't know. Shora, Kamla, Lakhmi, Kaama, Zaalai, I have sent for all your sisters. They are coming. They should come and see how bright our future is.' With these words, he hugged the son-in-law of his sister. Then he struck a pose as if someone was taking his photo.

The news had spread all over the tent colony, and a large number of people had gathered around Roshan Lal. His sisters and their children were hugging him. 'You have the good wishes of Arni. She will take care of you. You should remain for us, your sisters. Our brother's homes and our maternal home must remain alive.'

Usha felt bewildered why Roshan Lal did not talk to her. He was still annoyed with her. Her husband signalled to her and she dropped at Roshan Lal's feet, almost washing the latter's feet with her tears, 'Uncle, forgive me and relieve me of my burden or I will die right here at your feet.'

But Roshan Lal stood like a statue of stone like a statesman preparing to deliver a long speech.

'Let him speak. Let him speak. It would be good if he gives out a wail or two.'

Roshan Lal did not say anything. After some time, he sat down and began to say something slowly as if to himself, Earlier in the day Father was telling me, 'Roshan, remember, you have a big family. Although all your sisters are in their respective homes but don't think that your responsibility is over. After the death of Sarra, I am feeling restless. Her daughter Usha is as irascible as she was herself. God knows if she will ever meet her aims. She is your responsibility. . . . You don't have to worry. If something goes wrong with you, the whole village is there to support you. I have had a good relationship with all in the village. They will come before the relatives to be of help to you. Gulla Bhat, Amma Bhat, Nisar, Ali.'

Roshan Lal was saying these names from memory. The relatives and neighbours gathered there felt the last ray of hope extinguishing. His sisters began to beat their faces.

'He is still lost somewhere in his village in Kashmir. Now he is talking about the death of his father. Someone, please, for God's sake, take him out of this.'

'Dear loved Rosha! Our affectionate brother!' A general yowl arose there. They looked left and right for Bodh *Maam* for help.

Roshan Lal was standing outside the tent and looking in all directions as if trying to recognize something by removing a blurring veil from his eyes. On his face was a strange brightness.

A man summoned courage and asked him, 'Roshan Lal, where is that Kaakh, what are you talking about? It has been twenty years since your father died. Now your mother has passed. Did you hear, mother has passed, Arni has died! Your father had only seen the cool shade of his village in Kashmir, your mother saw both the cool shade of the village and the fiery wasteland of Jammu. Today you are free of both! Your separation is complete!'

After saying this, this man looked over all of them. They congratulated him and asked him to continue. However, when he saw Roshan looking through the people, through the rivulet and the gorges, through the sunlight and sky, looking afar at something, he did not muster the courage to continue.

4

Earth

(1996)

Abstract: *It is a story in flashback. The narrator and Jala Sahab (nickname Joal in childhood) are in Jammu recalling the game of tipcat they played in Kashmir before migration. They were three friends: the narrator, Joal, and Banna. There was curfew outside on the day they played the game and their mothers were worried about their safety. Then they saw a man injured on the carrier of a cycle. He had received a bullet in his foot.*

Now, many years after their exile from Kashmir, their homes are two mounds of earth on which Muslim boys are playing.

'May the blunted thorn pierce you!!?
… … … … … … … … … … … … … … … … … … ,'

I felt shy to say aloud the second line of this curse-couplet. Both Joal and Banna came running in front of me when they heard this line from me. Their movement up and down the ladder was audible in the whole house. If anyone moved up or down the wooden house with a heavier than usual step or quickly, all the props underneath the building shook. And our favourite game began.

'Go ahead. Keep the *potaej* on the hole quickly.[1] There will be curfew soon.' Joal said this while standing on the hitting mark and holding the stick in his hand.

On that day the schools were closed at 2 pm. When I reached home, I had reminded both, 'You owe me a ride.'

I had calculated that as soon as I complete my turn in the game, the curfew would be imposed. People were walking quickly towards their

---

[1] It was the longer stick in the game of tipcat. In villages it was called *loaeth* but in urban areas, *potaej*. It was used to hit the short billet of wood called *laethkij*.

Rupture. Rattan Lal Shant, Translated by Dr Javaid Iqbal Bhat, Oxford University Press. © Oxford University Press 2022. DOI: 10.1093/oso/9780192865083.003.0004

homes. The *tongas*[2] had already stopped plying on the roads. And meanwhile, a cycle had also appeared. The road was becoming deserted.

Fretcha Ded, Joal's mother, came shouting after her son, 'So much temptation has Nanna *Thool*[3] created in you that you almost slid down the ladder. Who gave you the money? Where have you delivered the milk?' She looked at me from the corner of her eyes while saying this.

'Wife of Harda Kaakh.... Will tell you later, mother,' replied Joal from the spot where he was playing and ran after the little stick which I had hit with *potaej*.

'Come, take out the soya. Shall we not eat?' Hearing the name Harda Kaakh's wife, Banna began to scramble in Joal's pocket.

'Hitting towards the rivulet is forbidden. You are finished! Your turn is over, Nanna!!!' Joal shouted from his place.

Joal turned towards me first and then told Banna earnestly, 'I swear by my mother, wife of Harda Kaakh did not give anything today. Even I was in a hurry due to the news of curfew.'

'Did I not tell you to remain placed a little behind? You would have caught the billet of wood!' Banna told him angrily.

I remember it all vividly as if the incident had happened yesterday. I said he had committed a foul in the game. I ran to see. I stumbled. The big toe started to bleed profusely. I slumped down right there. There was more earth than pebbles on the road. I gathered some dry earth and put it on the wound.

'Just pee on it all!!!!!!' Joal came running, angry perhaps at my accusation of playing foul. I held the big toe in my fist tight and limping and bending my back, I went to a wall to urinate. 'My turn is in the custody of the peer'[4]; saying this, I put the *potaej* down.

God knows how Fretcha Ded popped up and saw all this. She called my mother from the window, 'Arundhati! This wanderer of a fellow has done the deed!' Then she turned to me and said, 'Good for you!!'

My mother came beating her chest and took me dragging with my drawstring untied. A trail of blood was left on the road.

---

[2] A horse-driven carriage.
[3] It means, Nanna, the Egg; a nickname.
[4] This is the literal translation. What he means is that his turn is yet to be taken, and they have to give him. 'Peer' means a spiritual guide.

'When you tie him down at home, break his other toe and he will understand,' Fretcha Ded told my mother.

Then she began to search for Joal. 'You have defamed me, Jaelya, may a bullet hit your waist.[5] I know you must have made him hasten, and now made the innocent guy a bloodied figure.'

The shouts of Fretcha Ded in the silence of curfew! Banna's mother and some other neighbours started looking out of their windows. Bending low Banna escaped alongside our home and then slipped by the door of our courtyard.

Now the road was deserted and quiet.

And then there was a shout and people began to run. My mother shut all the windows from inside. I came down to see what was happening while trying to bear the pain. Mother hit me from behind asking why I had come down.

All the members of our family were watching through chinks and glasses in the windows. It was not easy for me to sit back. A crowd of people came by and went. Then there was silence. From a distance came a weeping cry, 'My dear mother! I am dying!'

A person on a bicycle with a middle-aged man on the carrier behind went by. From the latter's foot blood was oozing. He was the person weeping and screaming.

Fretcha Ded came out through the window. She might have recognized the man on the bicycle because he stopped. Or maybe he stopped for some rest; pedalling the bicycle had exhausted him and he was breathing heavily.

'The poor guy has received a bullet on the ankle. I thought I would help him.' The cycle man told Fretcha Ded.

Right then Joal came out swiftly and held the cycle with his hand from behind. It seemed the injured man behind was passing out and would fall anytime. He was writhing in pain and pleading with the rider to move on.

'Dear Mother, he is Harda Kaakh. I will support him up to his home.'

'Come inside! You will hold him up to his home!' Fretcha thundered at him.

'Let him hold him for a while. I have to come by this way when I return. I will bring your son quickly back on my bicycle,' the rider assured her.

---

[5] Joal and Jaelya refer to the same boy.

Fretcha Ded went inside. Our dilapidated home began to shake. She must have come down running from above. She appeared in front of the bicycle in no time. She had brought milk in a cup. With one hand she held the cup of milk against the lips of the injured man and with the other hand, she held his head.

'Damn with the quickness!! The reward for your good deed is with you, and you carry him. Did you not find anyone except Joal?' Fretcha's nostrils were flaring.

The rider looked all around. There was no one. He was lost for speech. From a distance he heard a whistle of policemen and the sounds of feet. The rider began to walk. Fretcha Ded also went inside quickly. Joal also got in but kept looking behind at the half-open door.

'Now why have you stopped behind there?' Fretcha Ded shut the window. Closing the door she said, as if to herself, 'The bullet has been fired.... What else would have happened? His foot got injured.... What else would have happened to him? What if this man is injured? What then?'

I heard this much. I don't know whether my mother heard that. I remember that she slammed the window shut and slapped me from a distance. I got rooted there like a statue. I don't know whether it was my pending punishment or Fretcha Ded's insinuation.

The policeman was hitting the road outside with his stick and inside all the family members bent their heads low as if they were thinking something.

Joal must have been receiving a beating. I was staring and our ramshackle home was shaking.

'Are you listening? On that day! My mother's slap had not done much to me but the beating I received from you pierced through my skin. I was thinking about it all here in Jammu and bearing it all.... I may also have had got marks on my body.' I told Jala Sahab. He had descended into some reflection.

Jala Sahab stretched out his legs. My daughter-in-law brought another pillow and handed it over to him. She placed it under his elbow. Keeping his head low he was gazing at my foot. After a few moments, he said as if talking with himself, 'How severe was the winter of 1993! We had lost all hope of grandmother. During her last few moments, she opened her eyes.' The colour of Jala Sahab's face turned black. His irises turned lifeless like two pebbles. 'Never forget to lock the two homes. Keep a watch on both of them.... As if she had held her life back to say these words.'

I was eager to go back, sometimes wringing my hands in anticipation of going to Kashmir. I could not dare to visit Kashmir even after hearing about the death of Fretcha Ded, mother of Jala Sahab, the childhood Joal.

He was continuously speaking while gazing at my foot as if memorizing a lesson.

'How on earth could I send you a message from Kashmir? Did I know your address?' He said.

'Did I have ... ?' I felt like telling him how for three–four years I was wandering in Jammu with a bag of utensils, from one rented room to another but could not gather anything to tell him. Looking at the muddy ditch of his eyes, I tried a lot to bring a smile on my lips. 'Did you hear Jala Saeb, here on our heads is not the old home of Kashmir, neither under our feet the old earth!' Saying this I gave out a burst of loud laughter.

But he was serious. I don't know how he managed to let these few words out of his mouth, 'Earth? Yes, there is now plenty of it compared to the old times. On the road, I mean. The road has turned into the Boulevard. There are a couple of pockmarks on her face but she can't help them.'

Two small pockmarks? I was just wondering what he meant by this when he explained, 'The two mounds of the earth of your and Bansi's home. Year after year they come down closer to ground. On those two my.... (he paused) I mean the children of Parvaiz Ahmad and Altaf play on them now.' Speaking like that he lifted his gaze and rested it on the moving fan on the ceiling. The fan had been gathering the hot air for a long time and throwing it down on us.

5

Fire

(1993)

Wish we had our soil, our composition
Who knows how long we will survive, who will begin to detest us?!

Rehman Rahi

Abstract: *Jagarnath comes to visit the family of Nandlal and his wife Shobavati in the refugee camp at Jammu. There is Nand Lal's son Chand and the latter's wife Chuni, and their daughter Daali. Their room is cramped for space. Their son Lal Ji has disappeared. Jagarnath tells them that an acquaintance of his has seen Lal Ji in Kashmir. But this seems to be a piece of fake news. The actual intention of Jagarnath is to prompt the refugee family to sell their house in Kashmir. This intention of Jagarnath psychologically disturbs the refugee family.*

Jagarnath pushed the door with great force. Both its panels shook with a loud noise. The curtain hanging from inside came off from one of the nails and stuck to one of the panels.

It was the afternoon of June in Jammu. Outside the room not a leaf was astir, neither was there any movement inside the room, nor any voice audible. The door opening in this manner was like a flame of forest fire entering a cave. In the darkness of the room, the family members had fallen almost unconscious. And the open door had pressed the air inside into motion.

Jagarnath could not enter because there was no space for landing his step in this small room.

Rupture. Rattan Lal Shant, Translated by Dr Javaid Iqbal Bhat, Oxford University Press. © Oxford University Press 2022. DOI: 10.1093/oso/9780192865083.003.0005

Shobavati was sleeping close to the door. She got up hastily, gathered up the *dhoti,* and covered her head. Rubbing her eyes, she was trying to recognize the person standing at the threshold of the door, who was neither coming inside nor going outside. Near the feet of Shobavati was Chandji. It irritated him a lot to see a stranger arrive at this inappropriate time. He did not get up. He placed his hand on his eyes trying to recognize the black statue of a man standing at the sunny threshold. Near his feet were Chuni, his wife, and Daali—asleep, close to each other, and wrapped in clothes. Chuni got up suddenly and realizing her clothes were in disarray, went to the kitchen to arrange them.

Even the crevices of the room had been closed with clothes and scraps of newspaper. They had made the room dark so that neither the daylight nor the fiery air would enter. The ceiling fan was twirling the air and sending down beatings of hot air on them. But they were used to it. They had become acquainted with that. The demon of outside heat and light was now inside with its mouth wide open as if to devour them.

Shoba felt it was Chand's father who has come with relief material given to the refugees. On the day of relief material distributions, he would be as if possessed by genies. She was about to reprimand him when a different voice filled her ears.

'Shobavati, this is me, ... me ... Jagarnath.'

Shobavati and her family members still unable to figure out which relative had come to meet them, were anxious why the door was not being closed. Their lives had been growing weary with the dream of cooling their bodies by rubbing against the bare concrete and wearing thin clothes. Now Shoba recognized him. 'He is jagarnath whose general behaviour is not different from what he did just now.' Chandji got up and picked an undershirt from a nail and put it on. He got a mat from the kitchen and spread it out on the floor.

Chandji closed the door, adjusted the door curtain. Now he began to recollect who this Jagarnath was; Jagarnath, who was easily recognized by his nickname name Jaguir.

Sitting down Jagarnath called out towards Shobavati who had gone inside the kitchen 'Shobavati, I was a lot disturbed when I came to know about the disappearance of your son.... Now I thought that since I have come to Jammu so.'

The mention of her son seemed as if someone had touched a raw boil on her body. A scream issued from her mouth. 'My son! My beloved!!.' Weeping, she sat in a corner with her head on her knees.

The door was closed as before, the curtain was spread out. The ceiling fan was also gathering hot air and pouring it on the family members. The screams of Shobavati made no difference to anyone or anything. Outside the room, the afternoon weltering sun had strangled the streets, roads, and houses. There was no sign of movement from anywhere. Not a leaf on a tree swayed. No sparrow stretched itself out.

Even as she was sobbing, Shoba made another scream towards Chandji 'Where has your father gone?'

The father heard in the courtyard. He had seen Jaguir going inside the room. He was also waiting for someone to call him. There was a tree in the courtyard that bore just thorns and blackened leaves. In the shade of this tree, he was sitting on two bricks. A lost human being, bearing the weight of exile, he would spend the whole day in the sparse shade of this tree and go from one wall of the courtyard to another. Sometimes next to the courtyard wall and sometimes to the left wall of the room-sized house, he would sit on those two bricks. The newspaper, which would have been read by Chandji by lunchtime or seen by Shobavati or his daughter-in-law (for the pictures of the dead), he would carry and spend the long day outside the room. At night he would not stretch himself or sleep on his side, fearing that it might be inconvenient to his daughter-in-law. If Chandji or his wife slept in the kitchen, they would lay his bed in the room. Otherwise, his sleeping place was also outside. For the last five years, this practice had become established. The stage had come when no one had any problem with this arrangement nor was it considered extraordinary. No question had come up regarding this nor had anyone tried to seek an answer.

Innumerable pebbles, scraps of concrete, and pieces of bricks had got embedded in the surface of the slam courtyard. The tenant of this room-sized house was every day making a small mound of these variegated pieces, tying them in a piece of cloth, and then throwing them outside near the road. Along with the promise of constructing the house, the landlord had said that he would grow grass on the courtyard ground. To remind the landlord after three years of the promises he had made was to create the problem of searching for another place to live in. The landlord took his own time, the tenant took his own time, and his family also did the same.

Besides, Nand Lal also did not seem to be in a hurry. He went on gathering the pebbles and passing on his days.

When he heard the shout of his wife, Nand Lal picked up the two bricks and kept them next to the wall. He had worn an undershirt and pants. He kept the handkerchief twisted in his pant pocket. There was no hurry so he stretched himself out. I know this guy Jaguir, and his ways, he told himself.

Meanwhile, there came another shout for him, 'Where is your father? Chand go and find him out.'

Nand Lal opened the door slowly and the shout from inside came like a fiery slap on his face.

'Are you listening? He has seen Lal Ji in Kashmir.... Hey, My Lal Ji! Your mother will die for you, Lal Ji!' She again began to weep.

When Jagarnath saw Nand Lal's face he did not like it. Wide-eyed and fingers between his teeth, he stood there surprised to see Nand Lal in that condition.

'So unfortunate!! Chandji! Is your father in his right senses? What was he doing outside in this blistering heat?' said Jagarnath. When Nandlal was about to sit next to Jagarnath, the latter sat a little away from him as if he might have been afflicted by Nandlal's condition. Nandlal began to blow his nose. Shobavati was slowly lamenting and Chuni was at the threshold of the kitchen door and waving at Daali with a page of the newspaper.

Chand gradually began to recollect everything. Jaguir was a wanderer, half-inheritor of a big old house and lived like the ghost of an abandoned bungalow in Kashmir. He had made a separate ladder for his part of the house. He did not permit his brothers, nephews, or their children to cross into his side of the courtyard. The mohalla had nearly forgotten about his existence. The people came to know about him and his being alive when some accident or tragedy befell his ghostly bungalow. He married a widow and brought her in along with her children. When they quarrelled or he beat her up, the people around would be reminded of him. Or when his elder child would beat him and break his legs and desert him. Then for months, he would be in the hospital. Who had time to go and find out whether he was alive or had died?! After six months or a year, a similar drama would unfold in that house. The police would come and the matter calmed down. He used to disappear for two, or sometimes four, months. Then he would come back and again the house would come alive with quarrels.

Jagarnath had perhaps sensed that his arrival was being ignored. He focused on Nand Lal, the soft target, 'The truth is that I have not seen him myself. There is one Salaam *Woakha*.[1] You don't know him. He had seen him somewhere at Nowhatta, Srinagar working with some baker.'

There was again silence. Nandlal is removing sweat from his self. Perhaps waiting to see who will answer Jagarnath.

After a short while there was a pause in the sobbing. Shobavati responded as if asking herself, 'When did he see him? When?'

Jagarnath was encouraged to speak by her response. He sat cross-legged and replied, 'Around three months ago. Even I did not get time since then.... On top of that this roasting heat here in Jammu.... And I swear—only a bastard will come here again in this scorching heat!'

Chand had begun to dislike Jagarnath. But he was not able to gather any words. 'What shall I tell him?' he thought. Right then his wife signalled him with her eyes to enquire of Jagarnath. With great struggle with himself, he finally asked him, 'You did not get time, *mahra*? Could you not even send a message through someone?'

Jagarnath felt more comfortable with the family's interest in him. He felt at ease and pulled the pillow from behind, a little low underneath him and stretched his legs wide and put one leg on the other.

Chuni had come with a glass of water for him. Just one sip of the warm water irritated him. 'Don't you put ice in water, dear Nand Lal? Don't you understand you will have to stay here for an unknown time?' he said wondering why they were not adjusting themselves to the situation, especially the hot weather and its requirements.

He had another sip and completed his observation, 'If you want to stay here well, live like the people who are already here. Yes, I am telling you! Otherwise, you will remain neither of this place nor of Kashmir.'

Chuni got another glass of water and gave that to Nand Lal. He kept on gazing at his daughter-in-law as if trying to recognize her. Actually, he

---

[1] 'Woakha' literally means terrible, dangerous. People are afraid of a person who is called 'woakha'.

was reflecting on the words of Chand. He turned his head towards Chand, 'You think I cannot go to Nowhatta. You won't understand! Listen! I don't have any restriction.'

Then he waved his arm as if making an announcement 'You made a big mistake in running away from Kashmir. If not a mistake, then what?'

Yes, when did it not seem that he was regretting his mistake? He did not even speak. He was looking at Jagarnath as if telling him, 'I have committed a mistake.' And asking Jaguir for the punishment he deserved for running away.

In the half-darkness of the room, the words of Jagarnath about adjusting to the climate in Jammu went about swirling aimlessly like smoke. Chand felt suffocated. He asked him, 'Where did you, *Mahra*, hear about Lal?'[2] He sensed that the question in this form is useless, and rephrased it, 'This Salaam *Woakha, Mahra*, how did he know about Lal Ji?'

Jagarnath was amused by this question and got up a little from his position. 'What are you saying Chandji? There in Kashmir, we come to know first and then you hear on the radio about what happened and where.'

The news was such that Nand Lal's eyes opened, and he began to talk, 'But you must also be frightened, that something might happen.' He sat down with arms folded about him as if coming close to danger.

When Jagarnath heard this, he spoke as if pouncing on Nand Lal, 'What are you saying? They warn me overnight not to cross over to Habba Kadal, or to go to Zaina Kadal, or if I am going to Lal Chowk, I should be back home earlier. We have to do *action* in that area.'[3] He put extra stress on the word 'action'.

Action, action, action. Chand felt the word, which echoed for a long time, whirling around the room with the wind of the fan and striking against the walls, making holes in the walls, bricks coming down and a pit created in the middle of the room from which Lal Ji was raising his hands and screaming, pleading to be taken out, 'Please take me out! Here even the earth under my feet is burning. I am burnt! Here fire is pouring out of the walls.'

---

[2] Mahra is an appellation term for Kashmiri Hindus. A short form of Maharaj.
[3] The word 'action' was used by militants for an operation against the Indian military personnel.

There was silence again. Perhaps hearing the name Habba Kadal and Zaina Kadal,[4] wonderment had descended on them in the room.

Nand Lal took out some pieces of pottery from his pocket and began to put them on top of each other as if making a tower.

Chandji came in front of Jaguir, 'I had only heard about it, Mahra. Today I saw with my own eyes how happily you are living in Kashmir.'

Jagarnath Nath retorted, 'How can we get back those days? Now I am alone in the whole mohalla.... I have made the whole region a region of peace.... Can't describe to you what my eyes have witnessed.... But despite that, I tell you one thing, that I am taking advantage of them.'

Jaguir slid aside. Chandji looked at his wife and addressed Jaguir but still looking at his wife. 'Yes, I know that!' Chuni returned the response with a glance, 'See how he is preening about staying back in Kashmir!'

Jagarnath took out a cigarette from his pocket and placing it in his mouth, asked Chuni for a matchbox. Then he turned to Nand Lal, 'Are you not smoking nowadays?' Nand Lal had wrapped the pottery pieces back into his pocket.

Shobavati was looking at Jaguir thinking he had not yet delivered his actual message for which he seemed to have come. To bring him back to the real purpose of his visit, she told him in a heavy voice, 'Now three years of this narrative of my son will be over. You are also giving information which is three months ago.'

'That is good. Let him stay there. As if no one knows.... You just let me go back to Kashmir.' He closed his eyes and went on taking draughts from the cigarette and enjoying the smoking.

Shobavati saw that Jaguir was slipping into lethargy. To give him the feeling that he was a close relative and not a stranger, she told him, 'I have heard two-three families of our Mohalla have returned to their homes.'

It seemed Nand Lal woke up from deep slumber. 'Jagarnath do you have any information whether they went back in private buses or government convoy?' With these words, Nand Lal turned his attention to something else. He was counting something on the tips of his fingers.

Jagarnath turned alert. 'Not possible that they will cross over to Kashmir. Who whispered this information to you?'

Right then the fan stopped.

---

[4] Names of places in Srinagar.

Nand Lal got up. He wiped his nose and made an announcement. 'Now the electricity will come at four. It has gone off for three hours.' And then he sat down.

To lessen the darkness of the room, Chuni took off the curtains of the windows and opened one of the window panels a little. Jaguir began to wipe off his sweat.

'Hell! This is hell for you here! What happened Shobavati! You have not left your miserliness even here in Jammu! The whole world has installed coolers, why haven't you got one here?'

Shobavati was feeling giddy. All of a sudden she began to sob and weep, 'My dear Lal Ji! In this baking heat, the poor boy must be suffering in the oven of the baker.'

Chandji reprimanded his mother. 'How do we know where and with whom he is? I don't think he is in a baker's shop.' However, Shoba's tears did not stop. She screamed, 'Book my ticket for tomorrow. I will search for him myself.' Then she began to lament.

Now even Jagarnath felt dumb. He was making himself understand, 'What happened to you? You are an idiot! Why did you have to talk about her son right now in front of them all?'

Chandji tried to console his mother, 'Kaakni!⁵ Till now how many times have we been proved wrong? Maybe this information is also wrong.'

Jagarnath vented out his frustration caused by his hasty and inappropriate remark and the spoiled atmosphere, on Chandji, 'What are you saying?! When did you search him? Which other place did he have to shelter himself? You do not know anything about the current situation. Whenever you hear a loud noise here you cower with fear and hide yourselves.... But nothing happens in Kashmir without any reason. I am not in a position to tell you everything. Otherwise.'

Chand began to feel dizzy. He saw his father had hung his head low, and making jerky motions in his dreamy sleep. One day his college-going eighteen years old younger brother Lal Ji went to buy medicines for his father but he did not return. Then a long and excruciating search for his whereabouts began; all around, inside the city, outside the city, searched the streams, scoured the forests, searched in the tiraths, went to peers, and tied threads at the graves of saintly people; brought amulets,

---

⁵ This is sometimes used to address a mother.

arranged Satta Devas[6] and the *havvans*. If anyone gave them any information, they went there to look for him. During the daytime they went like lions in all directions and at night returned like the jackals to their homes. Upset, they would sleep on hungry stomachs. All were narrating their experiences and articulated the distress they had witnessed with their eyes. People tried to console them and bring cheer to them but nobody brought to Shobavati her lost son. If anyone told her anything about her son she would only weep and the father would keep rolling his eyes as if searching for something in the ceiling. Neither saying anything nor doing anything. They were also told to search for him in Kashmir, but who would search him and where? People came to sympathize had a glass of water and got up and left. Nand Lal carried on his routine of picking the pebbles in the courtyard, putting them in a piece of cloth, and then dropping them near the road. Shobavati shrank in a corner of the room and for hours her colour turned pale.

So many events related to her son had happened. One day a person came and said that he had seen him in Himachal climbing a forest. He had seen him with a stick and a *loata*[7] in his hand. He believed he was exactly their son. He said that he had pursued him but lost track after some time. Maybe he had reached some higher place, they felt. When Shobavati used to hear this, she would look at Chandji and his wife with earnest eyes, as if asking them to go and find him out. Chandji, on such occasions, would himself be in great difficulty. 'What should I do and what I should not?' he would ask himself. 'Should I leave to search for him or not?' Experience told him that it was all futile. If Lalji had desired of becoming a Sadhu, his parents would not have allowed him to go on that path; they would have scolded him out of that but now after three years have passed, who was going to do what. But at least he would have surely sent a message of his being alive.

However, Chandji used to put away all his logic and leave to search for him when he found his mother, shrunk in a corner, weeping silently and his father gathering pebbles in the courtyard. On that day also he left for Himachal, and gathered information about the village where he was seen. For two days he stayed at the foot of a mountain in a Gujjar *Dhoka*

---

[6] A special kind of bread made for distribution.
[7] A round water pot, typically of polished brass.

and then he sensed it was useless when everyone told him that they had never seen any Sadhu around that village; neither was there any *tirath*[8] in that direction. For Chuni the long days of absence of her husband caused great pain. On the one hand, Nand Lal and Shobavati wept and on the other, a line of relatives kept asking, 'Has Chandji also left now? Lal Ji will not be willing to come with Chand. He is showing his youthful ignorance. He left without giving any thought to the whole situation. It is useless.'

Chandji, Shobavati, Chuni, and everyone else were at this time listening to Jagarnath with such attention as if someone had for the first time revealed something. Their minds were drifting from one thought to the other. Jagarnath turned the conversation in another direction, and said in a sarcastic tone, 'All Bhat Sahabs are making their own guesses by reading newspapers. Feeling excited when they read in the newspapers the names of their mohallas, villages and their cities ... and feeling convinced that there must be fire everywhere in Kashmir. Now who will tell them not to reflect too much on this, because it is all "politics".'

Chandji understood that if both he and Jagarnath stayed in the room for some more time, he would get angry. Outside there was a chance yet of the heat subsiding. He tried to get up but almost fell due to a dizzying feeling. His wife held his arm. He gave a strong push to his wife as if she were the reason for his suffocation. He uttered such a quick shout at Jagarnath that Nand Lal lifted his head from his knees and Shobavati shook.

'Jagarnath! Shall I leave for Kashmir tomorrow?'

It seemed Jagarnath was waiting for the same. He answered him with as much abruptness, 'Yes, you can. I will give you a letter addressed to Salaam *Woakha* so that he will assist you.'

Chuni was in the kitchen. Jagarnath had already looked in that direction a couple of times. When she saw him looking, she had immediately understood that the guest was looking for tea. She came out quickly when she heard the shout of her husband.

There was no effect of the shout on Jagarnath. He had lit another cigarette and opened a window. Looking outside the window he told Chand, 'But don't make that mistake!'

Chand was stunned to hear this and wondered what he had said a while ago.

---

[8] A sacred spot, pilgrimage.

'Who knows what you have gone there for? Had not Shauri gone there to take out her belongings?' said Jagarnath.

When they heard the name Shauri, all of them seemed to have woken up from sleep. Kamla Shauri, the Principal of Girls School, had travelled to Kashmir to release the salary bills of female teachers. The way she had been killed threw shivers down everyone's spine. There were as many merciless stories of her death as there were speakers.

Chunni had poured tea in the cups. After having a couple of sips, Chandji began to say something to Jagarnath, with his hand placed against his lips, as if there was a stranger in the room who was not supposed to hear this.

'Leave these Batta[9] stories and speculations. I saw with my own eyes.' After a few more sips he said 'I was on that day seated on a shop front and witnessing everything. Shauri was dragged to the road and then killed.' Taking a bite on the Kulcha,[10] he spoke again, after a brief pause, 'This was her destiny, her time to die had come, and her death drove her to Kashmir. Silly she was; if she had withdrawn salary, she should have left. Your house is in order. Why on earth did you come here?' I told her, 'I will collect rent from them. It does not matter who enters your house until you are not there. You just be patient. I know all three families who are staying there. Just leave it to me.' But she didn't listen, and then.

After the murder of Kamla Shauri no one had enquired about the house or contacted the tenants.

The room had turned as silent as a grave. There was neither the sound of Shobavati's sobs nor the tinkling of pebbles in Nand Lal's pocket. Jagarnath suddenly became serious.

'That is why I was telling you,' he facetiously hit on the shoulder of Nand Lal, 'Right now you are getting some money. It is about time that you sell your house.'

Chand had heard that someone had started living in their house. But the word 'sell' came like a fiery rod and pierced through himself. Shobavati was shaken. 'Oh my dear God! What shall we sell?' she said in disbelief. Nand Lal also appeared to be transfixed. Jaguir read on his face what he was thinking about.

---

[9] Kashmiri pandits are called 'Batta' by Muslims.
[10] A type of bread.

'Rest assured about the people who are living in your house. For them, only one man is enough. His name is Salaam *Woakha*. He will break their bones.' No one was saying anything. Jagarnath felt even more encouraged and told them, 'Also don't think that your house is in the same condition as you had left it. Instead of watching it come down brick by brick, is it not better that you.' Still, no one said anything. Only Nand Lal lifted his eyes towards his son. Jagarnath again placed his hand on Nand Lal's shoulder.

'You are lucky that I am still living in the mohalla. Twice I saved your house from fire.' Again there was silence as if all were heartbroken.

'But why don't you people say anything?'

Sweat drops had appeared on the forehead of Chand. He quietly sat down.

Nand Lal kept shifting his seating place on the floor. Shobavati had fallen quiet. She was watching what was happening but was not able to understand anything.

Chand got up and went in front of Jagarnath. His hands were on his thighs. Chuni feared he might say something inappropriate to Jaguir. She wanted to go close to him.

Chandji said, 'Jagarnathji, I will definitely go back and live in my own home. From there I will leave to search for my brother.'

Jagarnath felt Chand was not just making empty claims of return. He would definitely go. He held his arm and slowly made him sit next to himself.

'Yes go. Nobody will stop you! That is your own house. . . . Go and enjoy there. But you're like my child. That is why I am telling you. . . . Go and get a piece of paper and I will write for you to Salaam Woakha. . . . And it would be a good idea to sell the house out there. . . . Then leave it to Salaam Woakha. . . . Even if you tell him to go to hell, he will go there for you, let alone Nowhatta.'

Jaguir got up, opened the windows and the door.

'Why does one feel suffocated here? Suffocation, both outside and inside.'

'The electricity has gone off, Mahra,' Chand reminded him. 'You should go outside for some fresh air. We are used to it.' He pointed towards outside as if he was forcing him to leave.

Jagarnath had gotten his answer, and he got up. He cast a hurt glance at all those inside the room and left talking to himself. Chandji had held the door open and was standing there. Shobavati was trying to understand the situation, and Nand Lal was looking towards the ceiling.

The doors and windows of this dingy room remained open for a long time. The evening shadows had started to enter the room. The corner in which Shobavati remained used to be covered by darkness before other parts of the room. From her part of the room, Shobavati was staring at the ceiling, as if startled by something. Nand Lal was stealthily watching how his son Chand was walking to and fro in the room.

Chandji planted himself in the centre of the room. He asked himself what he was doing. Looking at his state, he began to weep. And then sat down.

Chuni was now trying to awaken Daali but to no avail. Then she sat down to gaze at her own feet. She saw that her feet had wide-open cracks in them.

6

Air

(1997)

Abstract: *Omkar Nath is living in Jammu as a refugee. When the story begins, he is returning from Kashmir to Jammu in a bus. The trip of his group to Kashmir was organized by an independent organization from Kolkata. In Kashmir, they were taken to various tourist spots. He also meets his friend Assadullah in the Assembly of people. Assadullah asks him to come to his home and meet his family members. Omkar refuses and promises to come next year. The word 'home' resonates in his mind. He returns to Jammu and is lost in thoughts. The incidents like 'civil curfew' and announcements from mosque loudspeakers, around the time of his migration, haunt him.*

Everyone had food at Ramban.[1] We might have travelled just ten to fifteen miles from there that a child felt thirsty, and then everyone appeared to feel thirsty. At one place along the road there was a little waterfall. The driver stopped the bus at that spot.

Omkar also came down.

A whiff of cool air blew as he came down from the bus, and he stretched himself. He took a long breath. He wished that he could take this air in his kidneys to hot Jammu and there distribute it evenly among his exiled people. He wondered why in buses, as in houses, the air was hot; and why these buses carried it every day from one place to another, wherever they go. To produce coolness, it is important that the air comes out of doors and windows.

Only two to three men went towards the little waterfall to drink water. The rest scattered around. Omkar felt that even these people must be trying to take in enough cool air so that it can last with them in the blistering heat of Jammu.

---

[1] A town on the Jammu-Srinagar Highway. The travellers often take meals at this spot.

Rupture. Rattan Lal Shant, Translated by Dr Javaid Iqbal Bhat, Oxford University Press. © Oxford University Press 2022. DOI: 10.1093/oso/9780192865083.003.0006

On the edge of the road, Omkar sat on a big stone and looked outwards. It was some narrow valley of the Bani Haal Mountain. Ahead of him and behind were high mountain peaks with their shadows. Only a few peaks here and there were covered with a blanket of the afternoon sunlight. A milky line of a brook was flowing below in the depth. Right across the brook on the other side, were a couple of waterfalls like tiny threads hanging by the tops of trees. Omkar thought that no matter what craggy stones, forests, or sandy areas come in their way, all these thin threads will keep coming down, and finally reach the thick milky thread below. Before they reach the brook, they will be hit by many an obstacle and violent turbulence but ultimately, they will reach down and gain tranquillity.

Omkar's attention turned towards his own self. 'I had also gone to find out tranquillity in Kashmir. What did I find there to bring along?' He got up abruptly. 'What had I gone there for? Why had I gone?' He began to reflect.

The five days in Kashmir had passed very quickly. The discussions which had been going on for a long time in Jammu was eventually felt by many to have reached a meaningful end. The members of the exiled Hindu community said, 'Let us go straight to Kashmir and have an interaction.... If Muslims are sulking against us, what is the cause? ... They should have come. They have not come. So let us go. One day or the other even estranged cousins have to face each other.'

Some even said, 'Forget everything, at least there is a free round journey, a trip for two-three days. Whoever will go, will find someone or the other of his native village present there. We will also come to know what they are thinking, about us and about the whole situation.'

These conversations were going on and we found that a group of people had arrived to take us to Kashmir. God knows from where they had come and who had brought them. Many people went with this group. There was a two-day assembly of people in Srinagar. Everyone was intensely watching for someone from their native village in the assembly. God knows who met whom but the speeches continued. Photos were taken. Videos were shot. The first day passed. Omkar came across Assadullah on the second day. He called out to him, 'Hey, Assadullah'. His call just disappeared in the milling crowd. He felt thankful that people were listening to the speeches and no one heard his loud voice. It slipped out of his mind that he should not have shouted like that. Assadullah would have remained thereabouts in spite of his shout.

His sleep had disappeared ever since he had heard those speeches in Jammu and seen the enthusiasm of going to Kashmir after many years. In his dreams, he used to walk through the markets of Srinagar as if he was not afraid of going anywhere even if dusk fell while he was on the way.

He did not dare to turn towards the streets which eight years ago led towards the homes of his relatives. When he used to tell anyone about his dream they would laugh, and the listener would become a fan of his. He used to feel grateful when he would wake up from the dream because that saved him from the pain of losing his way on the streets in Srinagar. However, the next day soon after a sleep he would find himself losing way on the same streets. The streets were well known but the rest was unknown.

He continued to remain in the same restlessness. Until one day he boarded a bus and reached Srinagar along with this group.

Assadullah had heard his call. He slowly made his way through the crowd and held Omkar in an embrace. He took him out of the crowd. 'Come, what are you doing here?'

Omkar asked him, 'Where?'

Assadullah gave his reply in a composed manner. 'Home, where else?' He quickly understood that Omkar was on the horns of a dilemma, because of which his eyes spun around in their sockets, and thus modified his response. 'To my home, and no where else!!'

Omkar Nath had left behind the hot refugee camp in which families were living in single rooms. After reaching Kashmir he did not believe that he would be confounded by something which came like a gust in his face. Home!! My home!! The words created a strange ring in his mind.

Earlier Assadullah had come to meet him at Jammu. They had talked a lot. Assadullah had understood and Omkar Nath had thought that he has to go to Kashmir. They talked in a way that the man sitting in front could infer Assadullah's meaning, and in spite of hearing the words clearly even the walls of the room remained ambiguous about Omkar's going to Kashmir.

Anyhow, he changed the topic.

'Assadullah, who has asked you to come here? We were told that entire villages will come down to meet us in the assembly, but here we saw nothing like that.'

Assadullah laughed, 'You fool! You believe in what people say? I came because of Baabi.' Omkar could not recollect whether his wife Usha had previously said anything to Assadullah. Then there was no chance of my coming to Kashmir, Omkar thought.

'Don't know where she had got my phone number,' Assadullah explained. Omkar knew how she became a lioness when there was any emergency, an emergency like that of a Hindu returning to Kashmir. At that time nothing is impossible for her. Especially when she feels that it is a matter of life and security. She must have begged with Assadullah on phone about Omkar's coming to Kashmir, and entrusted him with her husband's safety.

He cut an innocent figure.

Inside the *shaamiana*[2] a speech was going on. Due to the speeches and clapping even the buntings seemed to be dancing around with excitement.

As soon as the assembly began the people who had come from Jammu started looking around for their acquaintances. Having not seen anyone of his own had made Omkar's heart cold, but today after seeing Assadullah why was not his heart melting? He was introspecting about his condition. Meanwhile, Assadullah informed him, 'No one knows that this assembly is taking place here! Still, the authorities might have informed some people.'

Omkar was deeply thinking about the mannerism of his wife. At the time of departure from Jammu, she quarrelled with him and did not want him to go alone. She could not go with him. If she had also come with him then there would have been no one with her school-going child and the old father and mother-in-law?

Omkar said in a low voice. 'No, what are you saying? This Park is in the centre of the city. Since morning you think that not even the people living in this mohalla have received news of this meeting. Here, even a whisper would in no time spread from Amira Kadal and sweep across all seven

---

[2] A shamiana is an Indian ceremonial tent, shelter, or awning, commonly used for outdoor parties, weddings, feasts, etc.

bridges of the city.[3] Whether it was about gathering people or shutting down the shops in the market. It is very easy to assemble people.'

When Assadullah heard this, he froze. Omkar regretted his statement and wondered about the need of making this complaint to this innocent person. He held his hand and took him to a side and handed him a cigarette.

'Don't feel upset, Asdya![4] ... Not this time round. They have made a program of two to three days. This evening they will take us to the Mughal Gardens. Tomorrow some leader will host our lunch. From there they will take us to Gulmarg. Early morning, day after tomorrow, we will be back to Jammu. We will be numbered and counted on our departure from here as we had been counted when we left for Kashmir.'

'Mughal Gardens, Gulmarg!! Omkara, don't you desire to go to your home? You have come after eight years. I am not telling you to stay there but at least do take a look at your house ... Don't you want to meet Abba, grandmother, and Jameela. They have insisted on me to bring you along.' Assadullah told him.

Omkar felt suffocated. He was seeing on Assadullah's face three patches each of joy, passion, and coldness had occupied their spaces. Assadullah was insisting on my coming with him but somewhere in his self he was convinced that this dear friend will not come. Omkar felt a fellow feeling in the eyes of Assadullah. Omkar changed the topic and asked him 'See, going in this way will neither satisfy them nor will it satisfy me. I will come next year along with Usha and Chintu. This is my promise to you!'

'Okay, I will also stay here with you in this assembly. Will they allow me to stay with you?' Assadullah asked Omkar.

Omkar did not know what to tell him because he didn't know whether the organizers would give permission. Assadullah understood that the question had sent Omkar into a dilemma. 'No, you did not understand what I mean to say. I will reach here in the morning. I will be with you during the day time, until day after tomorrow. I will help you to your seat in the bus, and return home.'

---

[3] Amira Kadal is the name of a bridge in Srinagar. There are seven bridges over river Jhelum which flows through Srinagar.
[4] Asdya is the shorter form of Asadullah.

Without waiting for Omkar's answer, Assadullah left and the former sat down there on the grass for a long time until the assembly was over.

He was wondering about the warmth and passion which had occasioned them in Jammu before coming to Kashmir, and how gradually the feelings of fellow-feeling had petered out. Here also in Kashmir apparently warm handshakes were taking place but actually life was frozen. He shook himself and got up.

He thought that everyone was busy in guarding his skin. Everyone was interpreting the season and situation according to his own way, otherwise neither Jammu had melted with the heat nor had Kashmir dried up in the cold.

His head had grown heavy. Right then he went back to his hotel room and slept.

The passengers had come back and the driver was blowing the horn. Omkar had not perhaps heard the horns. When he saw the conductor of the bus coming running towards him asking Omkar to hurry, he also ran and jumped onto the moving bus. He thought if Usha were with him, she would not have allowed him to come out of the bus, leave alone board a moving bus. 'Don't know why women sometimes scream suddenly! Don't know why women start weeping and crying when men remain dumb, dissolving from within! Don't know why women first of all see the extreme of any matter and then begin to grasp the routine parts of the same! When Usha was scared, it was unlimited, and when affection aroused in Jameela, there was again no end to the same. Is it because these women do not find ordinary life available for themselves?' Omkar mused.

To see ordinary life Omkar roamed around the markets and mohallas on the next day of the assembly. He saw that the number of people had increased ten times and trade had exceeded beyond what he had seen in the past before he and his family had migrated. He wandered without talking to anyone, with the sourness which is occasioned by moving around like a nameless character and without being noticed. His state of being was unknown and unrecognized both in Kashmir and in the undersized refugee rooms of Jammu. The only difference was that in Jammu the smoke of the heated walls struck the throat and the eyes, and here the ice-cold faces of the ghostly dilapidated and abandoned homes of Ganpatyar[5]

---

[5] A pandit habitation in Srinagar.

were looking with a yearning towards him, asking to be touched with his warm hands. But where would he get that warmth from?

The next day Yaseen was with Assadullah. Omkar had successfully persuaded Assadullah about not going to his home. But when he saw Yaseen he was wondering how he could refuse Yaseen's invitation to visit his home.

'Now I will have to go to the village. I will return by the roll call of the assembly of people in the evening.' But Yaseen was talking to him of something else. After hearing about the Assembly, the whole village had become alert. They thought it was bad news. The Government was taking recourse to trickery by organizing this trip and assembly.

When Omkar heard that, he was impelled to say, 'Which government are you talking about, Yaseen? This is some independent organisation from Kolkata which has arranged this Assembly. I did not trust the Government from the very beginning. Still I came.... I thought.'

'You did well. In the same way you should sometimes make up your mind and come here,' Yaseen told him.

'Yes, that is right. But you should telephone me beforehand,' Assadullah said as if answering.

'You have to come to your home. You must come without any suspicion or hesitation in mind,' Yaseen told him.

'Now you've made a promise to us. You must also bring Baabi and Chintu along with you,' Assadullah suggested.

Assadullah and Yaseen were nodding at each other, and speaking one after the other. Omkar was wondering whether they had come to give him farewell. 'Has Yaseen come down from the village to inform Assadullah or has he come to inform me that going to the village today was not appropriate. After all both are my well-wishers. They won't wish me harm in any manner. They did not wish me ill-will even on that day, in the month of Ramzan, when soon after *Sehri*,[6] I had to leave in the darkness after locking my home. At that time Yaseen's eyes were brimming with tears.'

Assadullah had told Omkar, 'You should've picked some more material with you to use while you are out of home.' Omkar placed his hand on his shoulder and told him, 'I will be back here day after tomorrow. But right now, it is not proper for me to stay here.' Assadullah embraced him tight

---

[6] Pre-dawn meal taken during the month of Ramzan.

and told him, 'Aba and *Deid*[7] will miss you a lot, when they will come to know that you have left.' But it seemed that Yaseen had become impatient. He told Assadullah, 'Let him go now. If he wants to leave, let him go so that the poor one can reach some destination in daylight.'

It was known to Asadullah and Yaseen as well as to Omkar that neither light nor any destination lay ahead of Omkar but he had no other option than letting his boat out amid the storm of the time.

Omkar felt that his helplessness was same even after eight years. The market was bright and abuzz, but when he was faced by its realities, he felt vulnerable. He wished to talk like the old times but during the conversation the shopkeeper asked him, 'Tell me Panditji, when you came from Jammu? When are you going back?' In the auto-rickshaw the driver, who settled the fair after much haggling, asked him, 'When you are not tired of going up the slopes, why don't you start walking here? Why are you looking for an auto-rickshaw?' Listening to this, Omkar looked at him sheepishly, and said, 'Say whatever you wish to say, do whatever you wish to do, I would not have climbed the slopes of Jammu. But is there any corner here where I could have run away. Even if I had to, I would not have felt tired.'

When Omkar felt his head getting heavy, the bus had halted at Udhampur. The passengers had gone inside roadside stalls to have tea. He also sat on an empty bench. On the table was some newspaper of the morning. Suddenly he thought there might be a report of their Srinagar Assembly. After searching he found in a small column on the last page a mention of that bomb blast at the Assembly site during the night. Of what happened during the Assembly, who met whom, who expressed his experiences and in which manner, there was no mention.

'It is surprising that the news of bomb blasts is being given priority and given space on front pages. This blast had caused no casualty and had happened after the Assembly had concluded. What coverage did it deserve? On the same day, in different places, three major accidents had occurred, whose complete details were given.' Omkar felt that perhaps he was not able to think beyond his limited circle, or the world had changed so much. 'All around only progress is going on.'

---

[7] Grandmother.

The passengers got into the bus and saw him already there in the seat. To keep himself away from their questioning gaze, he was looking outside through the glass panes. He thought that in the earlier days the buses leaving Kashmir towards Jammu used to be mostly empty during the summer season but now it seemed the buses were full of passengers just as they were when coming from Jammu to Srinagar. Really, times have changed a lot. He wondered whether it was just his life which remained inactive and stagnant while the lives of others moved on. If nothing at least the climate had changed.

When he got home, only Usha was there. She saw him and went straight towards the kitchen which was actually a corner of the room separated by a curtain. He had anticipated such a reaction from his wife. He decided that he would not tell her now.

He stretched himself and lay flat on the ground. He was feeling very tired having had to sit in the bus the whole day.

Meanwhile his father, mother, and sons arrived.

'Have you reached back safely?' his mother asked him. Omkar was feeling sleepy. He just said, 'Yes.' His father picked up the newspaper, and as was the routine, sat near another wall and began to read. His son put coal in the press and began to iron his school uniform. The noise made by the iron disturbed Omkar's sleep. 'Chintu, are you going to school tomorrow?' he asked his son.

Surprised, Chintu began to look at him, and replied (speaking in Urdu), 'Yes. Why? Is there anything tomorrow?'

'Was just wondering whether there is civil curfew tomorrow, people were saying!' Somehow these words came out of him, and he turned to a side.

'Civil curfew! What is that?' Chintu was surprised. His hands stopped, and his grandmother shouted at him, 'Your pants will burn. Move the press.'

Then Usha thundered at him. 'Chintu, go to the electric linesman. Otherwise it will be evening soon.'

'God knows what they have done to it! Whoever likes gets on the lamp-post and connects his wire dropping down our wire.' Chintu's mother said.

'You should have come out right then and cut their legs,' said Omkar's father without taking his eye off the newspaper.

'And you will sit against the wall and without anything to worry you!' Omkar's mother replied with anger.

As she said this, Chintu shouted to his grandparents, 'Both of you, please be quiet.'

Omkar might have dozed a little. He got up with a start when he heard the shout. Rubbing his eyes, he started looking in all directions as if he had come to this place for the first time and was trying to identify the members of this family. Jerkily, he asked them, 'Were they again saying this on the loudspeakers?'

'Loudspeaker! Papa, what are you saying?' Chintu shouted.

Not only his parents but even Usha had come out of the kitchen and was dazedly looking at him.

'I am going.' Saying this Chintu went out of the room.

Now Omkar had lowered his head as if he was regretting something. Presently, there was silence in the room. And then Omkar's mother told Usha, 'Give him a cup of tea. He has returned torn and exhausted by the journey.'

Holding his forehead and head tightly in his hands, Omkar was looking all around. He had thought that upon reaching Jammu, not only his family members but the other people living in the colony would eagerly ask him about Kashmir. When they had heard about the weather and then about the village, they would say, 'We will also go to Kashmir next year.'

However, they asked only about his well-being, nothing at all about these things. Neither his family members nor anyone from the camp.

He was lost in his thoughts for a long time.

His wife was standing in front of him. With a cup of tea and kettle.

7

Water

(1999)

Abstract: *Kishan Lal and his wife Duura return to Kashmir after ten years. They have come to meet Rasheed's daughter Tasleema. Tasleema is mentally distraught ever since her brother Rafiq got killed with a bullet. Rasheed takes them towards Dal and tells the story of Rafiq's tragic death. He asks them to stay back in Kashmir, if only for the sake of Tasleema. The couple is caught on the horns of a dilemma, not knowing whether to stay in Kashmir or leave for Jammu.*

From the Tourist Centre in Srinagar, we did not hire an auto or a taxi but we boarded a regular service bus. We did not want anyone in the mohalla to come to know of our arrival. The bus dropped us near our mohalla and we entered our lane quietly. Duura drew her sari from her head down to her eyebrows. She caught hold of the other end of her sari and brought that up to her nose and hid her face. I put on a hat that I had brought along for this very purpose. The reading glasses were with me. I wore them on. Without looking left or right, or even talking to anyone, we turned near our lane and went straight towards the home of Abdul Rasheed.

The lane reached our home as well but our house was behind Abdul Rasheed's house. The mud-wall separating the houses had been cut at a place to make way towards our home. Their rear side faced our home.

We were walking briskly hoping no one would recognize us. The truth was that each moment I had spent away from this lane and this mohalla for the last ten years was inflaming me, my emotions were brimming. Someone was telling me from inside. 'Why don't you shout? *My dear mohalla, brother and sisters! I am here! Kishan Lal, Kishna, and I have come here after ten years. Come down you all! Hold me in a tight embrace,*

Rupture. Rattan Lal Shant, Translated by Dr Javaid Iqbal Bhat, Oxford University Press. © Oxford University Press 2022. DOI: 10.1093/oso/9780192865083.003.0007

otherwise, I will explode like a bomb.' How I was holding my breath! I muffled the sounds of my steps.

And Duura? She was walking with her head down as if she was in some deep worry. I had been telling her for a long time, 'Let us go to Srinagar. We will take a look at our home.' She gave just one reply, 'For me, everything was over when we fled from there at midnight. It does not appear to me we have ever been there.'

But how was that moment! She was beside herself when she heard about Rashid's Tasleema. She became restless.

I was also wondering what to do. And she told me, 'I wish to fly to Tasleema.'

She did not talk about the mohalla or her own home. She just repeatedly asked me to get up and take her to Tasleema. Now as we were walking towards Tasleema's home she did not turn her eyes towards any passerby. We did not even see anyone that we could recognize. The evening had arrived.

We were just entering the gate of the courtyard when we saw Tasleema sitting on the doorstep of the house. She seemed to be lost in thought as her eyes were staring at something. She saw us but there was no reaction from her. When we reached near her, she got up slowly. Her eyes had become like black pits. Her hair was dishevelled. She would always cover her head when she saw me. But right now, it seemed as if I was not there. There was no emotion on her face, no surprise and neither any sign of affection.

Duura held Tasleema in a tight embrace and a tearful cry issued out from her. 'Tasleema! What catastrophe has fallen!' Tasleema remained standing like a statue. She kept looking at me as if I was made of glass and she was looking at someone else through me. It shook me to see her in this state.

Meanwhile, Ammaji, Abdul Rashid, and Shafiq arrived. Tasleema held tight Duura's hand. Without saying or hearing a word, she took her to her room upstairs. Duura walked slowly after her as if spellbound. I went after them.

Abdul Rashid, Ammaji, and Shafiq also came upstairs after us. They asked me about our journey from Jammu. They asked several questions: whether we had faced any problem on the way, why we had not called them on phone, whether we had eaten anything during the day. All of them were talking continuously as if they were a machine and Tasleema was holding the hand of Duura and just staring hard at her. I felt transfixed, looking at this state of Tasleema, with her just saying cursorily 'yes' or 'no' to my greetings. I felt suffocated. The sorrow of Rafiq's untimely death which was until now just an absent speculation, was now a reality before me; Like a huge god of death in this room, holding each movement and voice of this room in his fist. Gradually applying the squeeze.

There was silence again.

In this state emerged the voice of Tasleema like the howl of a jackal from a cave. She pulled Duura's arm with force and asked her reprimandingly, 'Didn't you say yesterday, 'I will send Rafiq after dinner?' Then what happened, did he fall asleep there?'

When the family members heard this, they felt restless and it seemed that they wanted to change the topic but were helpless. With great difficulty, Ammaji turned to Duura, 'Duura! You are too much! You did not say whether your daughter-in-law gave birth to a baby. We did not come for the marriage to Jammu, are you angry with us because of that?' I immediately sensed that Ammaji said this to try to minimize the seriousness of the situation.

Now Tasleema began to laugh out loudly. She turned towards Shafiq, 'You are illiterate, Shafiq! Get up and accompany them to their home. Don't forget to take the torch. This electricity has gone out.'

Then she started adjusting her frock, stroking her hair, and then looking out through the window. I looked towards Rasheed. He had bent his head down. Ammaji was standing with her back against the wall and looking at the ceiling with stunned eyes. Duura was barely able to control herself and was weeping with her eyes fixed on Tasleema. But no one made a sound. Shafiq said something to Tasleema and held her hand and perhaps took her to the other room.

I noticed that whenever I talked about Rafiq's death, they tried to change the topic. Rasheed said only once, 'God had to do it.' No one else said anything.

We almost spent the night without sleep. Before my and Duura's eyes flashed Rafiq of six years and Shafiq of eight years, as they were eleven years ago; sometimes going up and down our stairs, or holding my hands, taking me out of the room and down to play cricket. The younger one, Rafiq, used to stay with Duura for a long time, telling her, 'I will help you.'

He would ask for milk in the kitchen and then drink it there. On the contrary, Tasleema would chase him all day with a cup of milk asking him to drink it but to no avail. Sometimes he would fall asleep in our bed and I would carry him in my lap to his home. The separation of ten to twelve years which had turned into that of centuries was now rewinding before our eyes like the scene from a film. Our house was visible from the window of their room. If anyone made a shout here in Rasheed's house, we used to hear that clearly on our side. For a moment I felt like opening the window to see my home. I would come down and see my home after ten years. However, this idea did not last. Right before our eyes was the same six-year-old Rafiq, racing around, happy to see us sleeping in his bed, in his room. Just then Duura said, 'Do you remember how he came on that day before dawn and woke us up by repeated knocks on the door, and told us that the month of fasting, Ramzan, has started. And why had we not got up to take the *Sehri*.[1] He had seen through this window that our lights were off.'

'Yes, how can I forget that? His innocent face does not go away from my eyes. How much he would have grown in these years, and what he would have been like today! Our desire to see him grown up has remained unfulfilled.'

'Then I had to tell him a lie. That we woke up earlier and had our *Sehri* in the other room. How excited were the children about keeping the fast on the first day? Are the children today the same as they were then? On the seventh day after birth both the brothers used to be bedecked from morning till evening. First of all, I had to feed these two with apple and egg-plant cakes.' She was reminiscing with a tinge of regret. 'They say that he was doing good business now. His father had handed over the shop to him. He was a brilliant child, running the shop as well as studying.'

'The condition is not now normal here, my dear. And then what do we have to do?' I reminded Duura. Her response, it seems, was ready. 'I know we don't have to do anything here. Tasleema is in deep sorrow. And why shouldn't she be? I feel that I may have to stay here with her for some time.'

After hearing about Rafiq's death, we had left Jammu without any plan or preparation. Neither of us was happy or willing to return to Kashmir. *What should I do, should I go or not, can I go or not?*

---

[1] The post-midnight meal of Muslims during Ramzan.

The sun began to rise and there was a knock on the door. It was Shafiq with two cups of tea. He did not say anything and left. There was the same seriousness on his face as it was yesterday.

I reminded Duura, 'Did you observe Shafiq? It seems he has changed a lot.'

Then came Abdul Rasheed.

'Get up Kishan Ji. And Baabi you also get ready. Today I will take you to *Tulmul*.[2] If we leave early, we will return early.'

Duura and I looked at each other. *Is this the time for us to go to Tulmul? Have we come for that purpose?* But Rasheed did not listen to us. He started his car. Tasleema and Ammaji remained unaware until we had left. I was wondering why Rasheed had literally thrown us out of his house.

On the way, Duura asked him, 'What was the compulsion for you to take us to Tulmul first? We would have come next year and taken time out to trip around.'

Rasheed's eyes were fixed ahead as he was driving a bit fast. Without taking his eyes off the road he answered Duura, who was seated on the back seat. The words were struggling to come out of his mouth between pauses, 'Baabi, you are naive. We must be thinking that you should not come here again.' Then he cast a naughty look towards me.

I don't know why I felt angry at Rashid's taking us out of his home first and then talking to us in fragments and hurling slurs at us. I also tried to provoke him. 'Don't say *we*, say we all Kashmiri Muslims are not happy to see Kashmiri Pandits returning here.' Having said that I waited for what he will say in response.

On Rasheed's lips emerged that smile in which I could discern both cleverness and helplessness. From the time we had met the previous day it was the first time his lips had moved in this manner. I felt some relief inside and placed my hand on his shoulder.

Without looking at me, Rashid said, 'If you have already understood, then why you are asking me?' Then he continued, 'Baabi, that is possible. We might think like that. But we can never think that your holy places like Tulmul, Parbat, and Shankaracharya will be unsafe for you to go there.'

I told him, 'Tell me the truth. Are you now free to think like that? We have long been deprived of the freedom to come here.' He sat down there

[2] A sacred place of Kashmiri pandits.

looking at me as if saying, 'Please don't impel me to utter so much of truth.' I signalled him to look at the road.

Then he turned a little backward and asked Duura, 'Swear by Rafiq, tell me the truth, during these last ten years how many times did you yearn to go to Tulmul?' Seeing that this question had almost caught Duura like committing a theft, he laughed out loud.

'Baabi, do I know you only since yesterday? Leave Kishanji. I know each nerve of his body, and am aware how eager he might have been about coming to Tulmul.' And then he laughed again.

It made me happy to see Rashid laugh in this manner. I also retorted, 'Come on, drive ahead, I will also count each one of your intestines.'

'Be quiet. God forbid. Intestines and nerves! .... Meeting after such a long time, are you now going to do this?'

Both of us laughed our hearts out to see that Duura had been provoked to this reaction.

After this, there was again silence. Rashid, who had moments ago melted like snow, had again turned to stone. And we had reached Nigeen. I and Duura had tried to resume the conversation but Rasheed was detained by some thought. He was just making little sounds in agreement and driving ahead.

After crossing Naseem Bagh when he turned right towards Teil Bal, I felt as if I was suddenly awoken. 'Where are you going in that direction?' I asked him with a quick motion of the body. Duura did not know anything about this way but she was also awakened and began to look towards me.

Rasheed did not say anything. He went on to drive. After a few minutes, he stopped the car on the roadside, turned off the engine, and came out. He also opened our window and said, 'Come down. Let us rest for a while here.' Durra's face was shadowed with fear and restlessness. She was looking left and right and wondering where we were. This was one of the forlorn banks of the Dal Lake.

'Don't panic Baabi. I will take you to Tulmul also.'

We got down from the car and sat on the grass. In front of us was the Dal spread like a dirtied blue expanse. As if it was mourning. For a long distance something murky was spread on the water which I had not seen even in my dreams. For the first time, I saw something like bubbles rising out of water-like I had seen during my childhood at Shihil Teng in Maar stream. Hundreds of questions sprouted in my mind and I was wondering what has happened to the Dal. Or was it some remote bank of the Dal? It shocked me to see this ugly face of Dal after ten years and my heart was seized by something. Suddenly I returned from my thoughts. I consoled myself thinking whether the water here was clean like a mirror or muddy, what influence would it have on that bank where the Dal is perhaps still like a sheet of mirror—a sheet that makes the beholder's heart clean and pure as itself.

On my mind is still that mirror-sheet picture of the Dal. Sometimes when I was in any serious discussion, I used to say that this mental imaginary picture of Dal is my creation. The listener would turn his face to the other side as if saying 'we've heard. Don't start praising yourself.' I used to look towards him like a dim-wit as if telling him 'I am praising you for preserving it in this state.'

But this common duckweed,[3] this sludge and these stream bubbles. Which Dal is this?! It is said that the duckweed seeds spread very fast, it might end up making the whole Dal crooked and a swamp. Lost in my thoughts I had gone far away from my immediate surroundings. On our left side was Zabarwan mountain and the peak of Mahadev wrapped in mist, slowly laughing at me.

'But why are you not laughing out loud so that I can wake up, coming out of this dilemma?' My heart began to scream but the voice returned from my closed lips.

Or was it Rasheed laughing slowly… 'Hope you did not think that I have kidnapped you?… Kishna! I also lose my way … wandering around in my talks. Like Tasleema I also feel like seeing Rafiq around me…. I am also weeping…. Sometimes I feel like seeing him cross the road and sometimes running away through the streets.'

I came back from my thoughts. Placing my hand on his shoulder, I said 'Rasheed! Why did you take us away from home early in the morning? We came to you and Tasleema. Otherwise, it has now been ten years away from Kashmir. We haven't come back to Kashmir to only go to Tulmul?'

It seemed that Duura wanted to say the same to Rasheed.

---

[3] The botanical name of this duckweed is Lemna Minor. It grows on the surface and is green in colour.

'Dear brother, since yesterday we are as if on a hot pan. We could not bear this grief. We thought we will leave back today itself. But seeing the condition of Tasleema cuts my heart. My heart is weeping, Brother! Your Tasleema has turned into a lifeless stone.'

Hearing the word *stone* Rasheeda began to throw pebbles into the water. The pebbles created a hole at one place in the common duckweed. But the duckweed quickly went to and fro and filled the hole. Immediately Rasheed would hit another pebble at the same spot as if a race had started between Rasheed and the duckweed. Will he make a hole or will the duckweed not allow him to make a hole?

Drop by drop tears were flowing down his face.

The Rasheed whom I knew for thirty years, one who was daring and bold, one who used to pick up quarrels for nothing, one who used to force people to speak in a strange tongue, today for the first time was melting like a ball of snow.

I would also have wept but I controlled my heart. I told him 'Rasheed, the condition of our Home is hopeless. You have to muster the courage. No one knew that we will be encircled in this fire. Who knew it would sweep us away from our roots?'

After a little while he said as if he was reflecting on my words and before speaking was measuring my speech, 'I was watching everything in an abstract manner. I was aware of everything. I had kept Rafiq covered under my *pheran* until now. Finally, how did he slip away from me?'

Rasheed was regretful. His face was in gloom. He had knitted his eyebrows, pulling them towards the tip of the nose. He had centred his eyes on the ground. Then he said in the same manner, 'He might have fled long ago. Along with the same friend. Maybe that was the good thing to happen to him as well as to us.' He lifted his gaze towards the sky as if searching for some bird in there. 'Death was inevitable for him. I wish he had died on some mountain or in some forest. We could not have even found his body. And his mother would not have remained in this state of regret.'

The atmosphere became even heavier than before. The bank of the Dal grew quieter. Duura sensed it first. She told him, 'Tasleema's condition is alarming.... She has to be taken out of it. She has to be taken to a doctor. I feel that she will be cured in Delhi.' A few moments passed and she said, as if talking to herself, 'She is convinced that Rafiq is in our home. She does not remember that we are not living there right now. I suggest she should be taken inside our house someday. She should be taken around the whole house. When she won't find anyone there, she will weep her heart out. The burden of her heart will become light.' By giving so many suggestions in one breath, it appeared that Duura was herself feeling strange now. She was looking towards me expecting me to second her thoughts. But on the other side, it seemed Rasheed was talking to himself.

'Nothing is going to change in her. Anyone who comes there, she tells them the same things. She tells the same things to that friend of Rafiq. Why have you come alone? Tomorrow bring him along with you.'

I told him, 'What then, you must make that friend of his understand. That is, take him into confidence.... You should tell all this to the doctor.... Sometimes a similar incident takes the patient out of the grief of the previous incident. Do one thing. Make that friend of Rafiq meet me.'

When Rasheed heard this, he suddenly got up. 'No, not at all. You cannot meet him. I will never allow you to meet him.' With these words, he began to say nonsensical things and began to walk to and fro on that scorched bank of the Dal. Finally, he stopped in front of me. 'Kishna! I hope you do not take it otherwise! It is because of him that I took you out of the home so early in the morning. If anyone had seen you in our home, that boy would have received the information today itself.'

I was looking with amazement towards Rasheed. He was shivering like a leaf. He slumped down right there. With a gesture, he asked for water. I was so lost for my senses by this situation that I went down towards the Dal to get water in my hands. Duura shouted at me and told me that the water bottle was in the car.

Rasheed was sitting down as if under the agony of a heart attack. After taking a sip of water he signalled us not to worry. I relaxed. He heaving a deep sigh and told us:

'On that day Rafiq was alone at the shop. Out of nowhere a friend of his came running towards him, breathlessly, and told Rafiq that military men were after him, and he must be hidden somewhere. Rafiq took him inside the shop. He took off a plank of wood from the floor and dropped him into a corner of the basement. He put the lid on top of that, and placed a matting as a cover and returned to the counter and pretended as if he had been counting money for a long time. Then the military came and inquired. Rafiq denied and made them understand that no one came inside his shop. The military searched and did not find anything there. They began to look into the shops on the right and the left side. They blocked the traffic on the road. Finally, the officer sat on a chair near the counter and Rafiq began to have a casual conversation with him. The officer took out a cigarette. The rest of the soldiers were scattered around.... Meanwhile, a bullet was shot from inside the shop. The officer received a bullet in his leg, and he fell there. The soldiers outside began to return the fire without stop. Rafiq had come to the outside of the counter and stood in front of the officer trying to figure out who fired at him. But he received a bullet and he fell like a felled pine. The shop was all topsy-turvy and in no time, it caught fire.'

'And that friend? The poor guy must have burnt inside the big fire-pot?' I asked him.

'That is what everyone was saying. But from where and how he managed to escape, no one could understand.'

Abruptly, becoming serious, Rasheed said, 'It is him who comes to us now stealthily, and begins to talk to Tasleema as if trying to glean some secret from her.'

'But dear, she is not conscious of herself, what kind of secret must she have?' I was wondering.

'He says that Rafiq signaled to the officer that he is inside. That is why he lifted part of the lid and fired a bullet.'

'Impossible.... Wrong .. ,' I spoke out, involuntarily. 'Then why would he have given him refuge? After all, he was his friend.'

'This friend had tried many times before to get Rafiq along with him.... Ever since he was suspecting him of being on the side of the military. For absolutely no reason ... Only God and his Prophet knows, but I feel Rafiq was innocent,' Rashid told us.

Duura was feeling restless. She used to get up and sit down, repeatedly but was controlling herself. Finally, she said to him, 'The one he was suspecting has departed from this world. Now why he is coming to grate the wounds of Tasleema?'

'There is not one plague after us! Maybe he now feels that the military is patronising us! And on the contrary, even the military is not getting off our backs. Their spies are also doing circles around us,' Rasheed said.

'And what does Tasleema tell this ill-willing friend of Rafiq?' It irritated me a lot when Duura asked this question. I thought, 'What will she say to him?' But Rasheed answered Duura in the same manner, 'She talks to him in a very confidential manner. Dear, how is he concerned about her calamity? He just wants to get some secret from her. At that time we are just dumb and speechless.'

Both of us were petrified. Rasheed was for a long time pulling out handfuls of grass and hurling them towards the Dal. The grass was gathering on the duckweed. After a short while, he said: 'Sometimes he comes late in the night and sometimes early in the morning before the morning call for prayer. He wakes us up and talks about some inane things with Tasleema. Sometimes he does not come by himself but sends some other boy. Whenever we see a stranger we feel like shrinking ... We do not dare to ask him, "Why you have come?" I am also aware that someday a military man will be after him and there will be a search operation of our home.'

I was shaken and reminded of where I was. I got up. I nudged Duura. She also got up. I looked all around me to make sure that no one was looking from any side. But it was the same scorched bank of the Dal. Far away, cars running on the road. Either they were going towards Nishat or towards Naseembagh. Rasheed also got up on his shattered knees and we turned back towards the car.

That same silence again descended in the car. Again, we were just compelling ourselves to speak and Rasheed just making some customary sounds. On the way to Kashmir, I had seen Duura either sighing or feeling glad after seeing the markets and roads which she recognized, wondering whether our eyes had really seen them again. Ten years ago, it was ours. Now it is not ours, it looks strange now. When we were going from Jammu, all of that was running behind us. Our eyes spread out to see, but we were not able to see anything. Until we entered back into our *mohalla*. Instead of going towards his lane, he turned the car towards our lane. After observing our amazement, and without our telling anything to him, he addressed Duura,

'Baabi, I will definitely take you to Tulmul. Also, I will take you to Parbat and Shankaracharya.... But please forgive me this time.' Saying all this he took us close to our house, from the front side. He took out the keys from his pocket and opened the lock. The surrounding houses were also empty like that of our house. I thought that for the first time in ten years a car stopped in this quiet mohalla near our house and the gate of our house was opened. There was a long screeching sound and a couple of people in the far off homes seemed to have been awakened. The people living around were sticking out their heads through the windows and looking at us.

Standing outside the car I was trying to understand why Abdul Rasheed brought us here and what he was doing. I did not know about the state of mind of Duura, but I was afraid. I was frightened of entering my home after ten years. As if Rasheed was doing some illegal activity by opening my home and as if I was responsible for this. I felt that around me the homes were not quiet but it seemed as if for nothing from nowhere a forest of guns has stood up and I did not have any way to flee. Durra had not even come out of the car. She was slowly weeping.

When I saw the condition of the home, I was shocked.

Rasheed held Duura's hand and took her out of the car, and almost dragged her inside as if she was a patient returning home from the hospital. However, she dropped down on the doorstep.

Rasheed told me, 'Right now I will get just the kitchen and a room on the first floor cleaned. Then we will gradually begin the repair work. You will stay. Tomorrow or day after tomorrow, I will put men to work.'

He was speaking fast, not giving me my turn to speak. Like a child, I had lost the sense of balance about everything. I was not able to figure out what I should say. We had not mentioned our home even tacitly or by chance. The two of us, husband and wife, did not have a home even in our mind, let alone staying there. When we had left Jammu for Kashmir, there was only one idea in our mind. Somehow if we could reach near Rasheed and Tasleema and just.

Rasheed told us to wait there and he began to leave. I was looking at Duura and she was looking at me. Both of us were bewildered. We had landed in some strange and unknown place where no one was our own. Our condition was like that of those forest animals which are captured alive by the honest and sympathetic police of the Western countries from the baiting hunters and then carried in covered vehicles and put in some other forests. They must get confused like me wondering why they were brought to a strange forest, and why were we captured in the first place.

I caught hold of Rasheed's arm. 'Rasheed, listen! Please tell us what do we have to do here? Who told you to start the repair work here?'

Duura also got ready to speak, 'Dear, I have left home in haste and I have locked only half of the doors. When we left for Kashmir, I told the landlady that we would be back from Kashmir in two or three days.'

Rasheed turned back. Now he was neither a stone nor a snowball. He smiled a little and placed his arm over my shoulders. Then he told me with great earnestness, 'Today you have come to me after ten years. Now can't you do this little bit for me?' Then he looked at me as if waiting for my answer.

I was not able to understand what I could do for him. Duura was looking scared as a deer, looking intensely at the gloomy atmosphere, and then appearing to tell me. 'No, no, we will not stay here. This is not our place. All of this vanished on that day. All the relationships which emerged from this home, have all ended. No, I am not tempted by seeing my home. I will not stay here. I hope you will not also feel tempted by this home.'

Rasheed told both of us, trying to make us understand, 'No one can stop you from coming inside your home and living here. And no one is going to suspect you. After a few days, I will bring Tasleema here. Baabi, you said that she should be brought here.... For her sake you have to stay here.... Will you stay?'

Duura was looking towards me as if asking me to answer his question.

After some time Rasheed got his car inside our courtyard and locked the gate from inside.

Rasheed had asked us a question. Without hearing the answer, he passed through our courtyard, behind the house. There was a path to cross over to his own house. While leaving he had signalled to us that he was going to his home, and asked us to go along with him.

Today after ten years we were standing near our home. We were lost for the next move that we had to make.

Duura was looking towards me. Her quiet eyes were asking me, 'What do we have to do?'

I was passing my gaze from Duura to my home and then to Rasheed's home, and releasing a question into the air, *What do we have to do?*

I saw Tasleema come out of her window and looking right and left, at our courtyard and our home, and trying to look for us as if she was not able to locate us. Durra was looking at her and then at me and in between towards her strange-looking home.

8

Measureless

(1996)

For ages your and my blood is
Searching together
The calm of the bottom of the ocean
Or the sparks of hope in the blue sky,
But often hits the sharp stones of wilderness due to our haste
And they feel the cool with the blood of our feet.
Sometimes with patience amid the enchanted stones
Becomes the wait of the prolonged ages.

(Shafi Shauq)

Abstract: *The narrator recalls dreaming about Kashmir. He dreams about the boys playing around his home. He recalls the days when earthquakes occurred and how the people moved around. Now that he is in Jammu as a refugee he wakes up from strange dreams. Sometimes these dreams used to give him nightmares. However, things have changed now. He has got used to the situation in Jammu. He gets nightmares, family members reprimand him for disturbing their sleep, and life moves on. Or does it?*

I remember those days when I used to shriek at night, wake up, and stay sleepless on my bed. I used to sip water from the bottle kept on my bedside consoling myself that it was a dream. Now I am alive and safe in a rented building at Jammu far from that dangerous incident that happened in Kashmir and which woke me up from sleep.

Rupture. Rattan Lal Shant, Translated by Dr Javaid Iqbal Bhat, Oxford University Press. © Oxford University Press 2022. DOI: 10.1093/oso/9780192865083.003.0008

Now I don't dream of such incidents, whose interpretations were neither available in any *janthar*[1] nor were explained by our grandparents. All family members would gather around me when they heard me shriek, helping me with a glass of water, one pressing my shoulders and another caressing my forehead, saying, 'Don't worry, come out of your dream, rub your eyes, and return to your normal consciousness.' Then they would return to their beds for sleep even as they were whispering something among themselves. They would get very angry because this used to happen to me every two to four days. They used to talk in a low voice but Asha, sleeping beside me, growled at me, 'You spoilt our sleep. After all what has happened to you?! The whole world is snoring and you are shrieking out.'

Why would I not prefer snoring if it was up to me? Why would I then let dreams of the old mohalla of Kashmir, left behind fourteen years ago, haunt me? Boys which I seem to know and recognize—either trying to climb the windows and walls or calling me out by name to the road. I walked with them and the journey of escaping their traps and running over the hilltops started in my dream. I felt myself walking over the unknown paths. But actually all this journey was occurring in the room where I lay dissolved in a corner.

Asha used to remind me, 'Your mind is in some kind of discord. God knows what you are always thinking about. You used to keep yourself to your room in Kashmir and you are doing the same here. How many times did I tell you—shake Kashmir out with all your heart as I have done? Why don't I dream of Kashmir?'

Sometimes when Jiga visited us with her children, the dream would repeat, waking me up in the middle of the night. Asha would say, 'See, you have spoilt their sleep too. Why don't you say what you see in your dreams?'

'Yes dear, you will feel better and light-hearted if you share your dream with us,' Jiga insisted

'Why are you wasting your time on him? I am tired of asking, he never answers.' Asha, her mother, would tell her and the conversation about my dreams used to get nowhere.

---

[1] An amulet, a talisman.

I was a fool doing awful things during the day and touring the same absurd world at night.

I used to travel around. Perhaps I never wanted to leave and forget that old world of mine. Maybe these people were telling the truth because I also realized that that world was the world of my foolishness. After waking up it was not worth telling anyone, about that world.

Some strange roads, those I have never walked on even during the days when I had my wits about myself. It would start right from my room taking me to some unknown hills, to the meadows, dragging me towards the roots of chinar trees or willows, where I found myself scrambling some colourful flowing streams. I slipped and I drowned in the water.

Ten horses bound to a tonga with dozens of passengers travelling on it. In the middle of the road at some terrifying place a muddy shed where it is compulsory to stop and take rest. The tonga driver releases the horses and they move right and left towards the paddy fields. Some passengers enter a shed and come out with rods and beat me asking, 'Why did you get on this tonga. Where are you going?' I see the horses turn into bulls and the people busy ploughing their fields with the help of these bulls. I feel happy that they will not now look at me, and I run away. I am soon reminded of no longer being a resident of Kashmir. My home is not here. The evening has come, where will I go and then I suddenly wake up.

Now if I share this with anyone, he will tell me it was nice to run away from the danger in my dream and its interpretation is great—but why did I shriek and disturb the refugee colony in the middle of the night?

Asha gave me a nice piece of her mind, 'Listen, do one thing. It won't make any difference to you if you won't sleep all night. You sleep a lot during the day. And generally, most of the night you go sleepless. You are a kind of night-spirit, without any sleep!'

But those days have also passed. Now my private world is not afraid of such nights, nor do I now crave to see those chinars and willows.

My world is no longer that absurd.

Or is it the same condition? It may go away during the day but where will it go at nights?

Yesternight was too hot. The heat has continually increased for the last three months. Half of the monsoon season is over but there is no sign of rain. People are ailing as if they have lost their consciousness because of being doped. Under the fan which is throwing down hot air, half-conscious people toss and turn.

Suddenly the fans stopped with a quaking jerk. All around the coolers stopped functioning abruptly. Within no time the rooms turned into ovens. It was hard to breathe and everyone just got up. They left the rooms and moved to the lawns or went up to the rooftops. It was a fearsome and hot night and it appeared at someplace the silence was choking their throats. Mothers were caressing their little children who just woke up half asleep. And soon the world was filled with a chirping noise. Young boys started playing cricket on balconies. Some came up with teacups in their hands. Some tried to lay cots on balconies for sleep.

Just as I used to run without looking left or right when an earthquake struck in Kashmir, I was running the same way here and had reached the rooftop. Then I realized what was happening and saw the house owner's whole family there. 'Where is my wife?' I hastened downstairs. I saw her holding a candle in her hand searching for something randomly among clothes in the cupboard.

'You saw my green maxi anywhere?'

She was all awash in sweat. She said, 'Are you in your senses? You went up-stairs just wearing your underwear.'

I wondered she never cared about dress even when she left for the market. And now in this hot weather why had it caught her attention? I told her several times not to wear a red petticoat or a white blouse under a blue sari. To that, she returned, 'I am okay'. Before leaving for a wedding function one day I forced her to have a look at the mirror. 'See, your hair is looking dull and frizzy.' She just jerked her head, fondled her hair, and left the room, 'Let people call me a madcap. What then!' If she met anyone by the road, she would talk for hours with them hardly caring that the person accompanying her may have got tired and bored. Whether it is the mar-riage of a Kashmiri neighbour or a Dogra, she would spend her whole day there. Whether they ask for it or not she would still provide a helping hand in one or the other way. Forgetting her age, she would crack jokes with the bride and the little girls. Don't know what has happened to her after coming here?

I was thinking about all this and wearing clothes. In front of me she wiped her sweat for the third time and asked, 'Now why did you wear *kameez-shalwar*?'[2]

Maybe while thinking about her I was actually thinking about myself. Or maybe I was not thinking at all. I was just wearing my clothes. Now that she had asked, I had to answer.

'I am going to visit Jiga. I will bring her children here. Electricity has gone out. They will be feeling uneasy like the restless fish on a hot pan.'

No matter how much inattentive she might have been but after listening to my answer she came quickly to her senses. She asked, 'Now? At midnight? Will you go on foot? You will face the dogs and there are also gunmen on the way. You will create panic in the whole colony there. They will think of you as a thief and will beat you up. I guess you mistook my calling you a night-spirit as a compliment. Then you were rambling about all kinds of things because of a bad dream but right now you are wide awake. Or are you not fine?'

Oh! She asked me about everything. If only she asked me about the reason for going there. She could have felt quiet. Now I could not hold myself and gave her a dressing-down, 'See, they don't have a balcony, where they could go when the electricity goes out? The balcony belongs to the tenant on the upper floor and the landlord. The tenants of the two lower floors move out into the street. And the streets are spilled over with the dirty water of the drains. They don't have cots to take out with them. Little children! At least they will get some rest here.'

I could not speak much and had not been able to change her mind completely because she just came forward and leaned at the door to stop me, 'Why did you then have to wear this shirt and trouser? You will not feel hotter on the way in this dress? You have to walk two to three miles. Listen. Just wear your underwear and go. Actually, rub oil all over your body so that you will shine like a star in this night.'

And saying this, she sat down laughing. And there she rolled about.

Now I knew what to do in this situation. I got a water bottle and helped her drink some. Then I stayed for long beside her, fanning her with a hand-fan till she was asleep.

---

[2] Shirt and trouser.

Now I had also come to a stage where one can survive only by articulating the feelings of others. When a problem suddenly arises, you also find a solution quickly and the results too arrive fast whether that condition arises due to the absence of electricity on a hot summer day or due to an earthquake in chilly winters. Lack of electricity on a hot summer night leaves a person restless and sleepless, and he tries to find a way of running away like he does after having a nightmare. The only difference is that after the electricity has gone out, people here in Jammu leave their rooms and move up to the balconies and after the earthquake used to hit Kashmir, people came out from their rooms and moved out to the lobbies,[3] waiting for good or bad times.

I remember in the old *mohalla*[4] in Kashmir, houses were adjacent to each other and did not have big courtyards or gardens. If there was a big courtyard or garden, it was not such that we would come down there and remain safe at the time of an earthquake. I have been removed from my mohalla for fourteen years but the memory of the earthquake still shakes me here in Jammu and those sounds continue to haunt me.

'All praises to God! All praises to God!'

Those creaking sounds of the homes at night.... of the loose wires... weeping cries, the noise of the animals, and then a couple of minutes elapsed, the noise gradually subsided and the people slowly to their homes. Mother coming down with a jug of holy water and sprinkling it on the entrance to the house. Praying!

'We apologize for our mistakes. Please forgive our sins. Have mercy on our newborn children. All praise to the Lord!'

And then when night-spirits, who had come to drink water, left our homes and returned to the heavens, everything used to get better and peaceful.

My mother could never convince me when, as a kid, I asked about these spirits. 'Why do these spirits come here only at night, drink water, cause earthquakes and terrify us?' Though I had experienced earthquakes during day time, I believed all my life that those spirits that live in a world

---

[3] The Kashmiri word 'wuiz' does not actually translate into a lobby. It is a space that leads into various rooms of the ground floor, on the right or the left, or both the sides. The lobby is the closest equivalent.

[4] A part of the village.

other than ours slept during the day and stayed awake at night. During the hot nights, feeling untimely thirst they came to our world to quench it.

The noise inside the homes used to subside but on the roads people moved about. After every night-earthquake we used to hear a call from the road, 'Hey Kamli, Are you people fine?'

It was the voice of the maternal uncle of Aali Kadal,[5] who used to come up to our place to see his sisters and cousins.

Mother would reply from the window, 'We are fine, how about you? And how are others around there?'

After greetings, he would update us with the news about the damages caused by the earthquake.

'Merchant Nabir from Fateh kadal[6] — his home broke down. A woman from *Gaada Koacha*[7] fell off the stairs and was taken to hospital on a *tonga*. Down the Bana Mohalla in Razdan Street the electric wires have snapped and fallen to the ground. Young boys were rushing to the grid station to confirm why the electricity of their colony was not cut off at the time of the earthquake.'

Saying this he would start leaving but his sister pleaded with him hand-folded to come in. Then she would enter the house and sobbing, 'Someone please ask him why he is going from door to door in the middle of the night. The earthquake has hit everywhere and everyone has returned to their house frightened. The word of God is on everyone's lip. Why are you wandering like a night-spirit without any sleep?' I could not understand this night-spirit then nor am I able to understand it now.

Now it is over fourteen years and our minds have become used to the situation. Today if the electricity goes out, it doesn't matter. Let earthquakes hit, no worries. Let those known boys visit me in my dreams, take me out of my room, and make me walk the unknown paths, I will walk carefree because I know after moving those long distances, I will still be shrunk in one of the corners of my room. All that will happen is that I will shriek out and my family members will accuse me of disturbing their sleep.

---

[5] This is the name of a place in Srinagar. The word 'Kadal' means a bridge.
[6] Name of a place in Srinagar.
[7] Fish Street.

9

Dry Stream of the Camp

(1993)

Gather my scattered fragments,
Assemble my unraveled threads.

(Moti Lal Saqi)

Abstract: *Jagarnath and his wife Kamlavati are living with Indravati in a cramped refugee tent. Indravati is the mother of their daughter-in-law, Veena. Jagarnath and his wife suspect that their son Teja has abandoned them at the behest of his wife and occupied the room allotted to them by govt. Indravati also feels that her daughter is not caring enough. Indravati's son Pupa hears Jagarnath say that he would throw his son out of the room and also take the ration card. Pupa disappears after a rainy night. After return, he gives the reason why he had disappeared. He had gone to inform Teja and Veena. He could not reach there because the bridge had been washed away. Jagarnath denies having said this and watches the volume of his voice from that day onwards.*

Two to three days passed. The sky was covered with thin strands of a cloud. The heat continued and along with that, there was perhaps an illusory sign of the forthcoming rain. Eyes would spontaneously rise towards the sky wondering whether there was an intimation of the monsoon rain.

It was night time. Due to intense humidity, no one was able to sleep. On the camp of this steppe, people used to sit outside the tents for long hours as if praying for the monsoon rain. Sitting inside her tent Indravati was ruing her bad luck.

Rupture. Rattan Lal Shant, Translated by Dr Javaid Iqbal Bhat, Oxford University Press. © Oxford University Press 2022. DOI: 10.1093/oso/9780192865083.003.0009

Jagarnath had closed the flaps of the tent on both sides. There was an opening only behind the cooler so that air from outside could enter. On the other side was another opening for the air to leave. The coolers used to bring air from outside which Indravati felt was hotter than the one inside. But she did not dare say anything to him because he was the father of her son-in-law.

For his wife Kamlavati, Jagarnath had closed all entry points and corners of the tent because she was scared of the snakes.

Indravati was not afraid. She had been living in this tent for the last nine years along with her children. She never closed the tent. The snakes and scorpions came, so many died due to snake bites. What would they have done to her? Her husband had already given his life (for the community). For all the people. In Kashmir.

She did not even have a cooler. It had been installed by Jagarnath. The cooler used to be towards Kamlavati during the night. But Indravati never told him anything. It was not a big matter. She had an old cooler which she could have easily repaired. But where in the tent could that have been put? And then it was not proper to try to become level or equal in privileges with the parents of her son-in-law.

Indravati was sitting on her bedding.

Kamlavati's eyes were closed but she was not asleep. She was internally wondering about Indravati's gripe which caused her discomfort during the day and did not let her sleep at night. She also knew that in the morning she had to listen to her cries because she could not sleep at night, that she had headache and pain in the legs. Actually, she felt she knew the kind of pain that she had. She turned in her bed slowly.

Kamlavati saw that the hair of her husband was looking dishevelled. He looked very weak. What could the poor fellow do? In spite of being the father of the Indravati's son-in-law he had to be at the service of all. What could he do? This was his luck.

From the cooler came a cool waft of air. Indravati wished to lift the curtains. But the thought came quickly that, after all, these were in-laws and she had to behave properly. Slowly, without making any sounds, she returned to her bed.

Still, she felt restless. She thought that she should turn Pupa so that the cool air of the cooler can come to his face. Even the cooler seemed ineffective. It was running like a water mill. *Khatkhat... khatkhat.* Pupa must have been all sweat. But what could he do? She did not dare to change his position.

Jagarnath and Pupa slept on a wooden plank in a corner of the tent, and these two women slept on the floor. That was the total space in the tent. During daytime Jagarnath used to teach Pupa and Indravati appreciated that. That was the only benefit she got from her son-in-law's family while living with them.

Perhaps a wind had started blowing outside. The shreds of the tent had begun to flutter. If this wind had blown before the arrival of Kamlavati and Jagarnath, Indravati would have got up with her children. She would have patched up the holes of the tent with old pieces of matting. She would implant the stumps deep, tighten the ropes, and make the water channels around the tent deep. She had become used to this. The weather here in Jammu was uncertain. One moment there was no expectation of a drop of rain and the next moment there would be a river poured down. It used to impulsively come of her, 'Wish the storm of that kind may not strike anyone, neither Hindu nor Muslim.'

Kamlavati was awake. Even she could not sleep. She would look towards her husband and a deep sting seized her. She would be angry at him, and also pitied at him. What could the poor fellow have done?

When the two were almost thrown out of the room by their son and daughter-in-law after a covert consultation, the couple became speechless due to grief and surprise. Why only these two, at that time even the best would have become wordless. Soon after the marriage, these shameless people argued for the room. *Why didn't they go out for a rented room? No. What a trick they played and pushed us to this shredded tent.* In that camp there were many conveniences, here they were in wretchedness.

Indravati sensed that Kamla was awake. She remained still and silent in her bedding so that Kamla was not touched and would not realize that she was awake. She did not have to utter even a word. There was no other option; otherwise tomorrow she would curse the tent and say bad things about her daughter. 'What is the fault of my innocent daughter? After marriage she asked her in-laws for the room, so what wrong did she commit? At that time her husband seemed naive. He should have asked his mother for a room before his marriage. Or did he want to put a spinning wheel between them like his parents did? On one side sleeping with her husband and on the other side her son with his wife.' She felt saddened and slowly turned in her bed.

Far away there was a clap of thunder and Jagarnath woke up. He got up and switched on the torch. He checked the time. It was 2 am. He saw that both women were asleep. He got up quietly. He turned Pupa to one side. He opened the rope, lifted the curtain, and went outside the tent. He looked all around and heaved a sigh. He wished for a ruthless rain so that the ragged tents are shattered. He thought, 'Had he not been thrown out by his son, he would not have come here, to this wretched place. This camp on the steppe was that of god-forsaken people. There was not even a sign of any thorny bush on this steppe. There is a stream and even that is dry. The people are without brains in their heads and tongues in their mouths. They could never do anything here. On the other hand, is our camp below. The ground is flat. There are plants and trees. There are all kinds of facilities given to us there. However, my luck was bad. Teja lost his brains because of his talkative wife, otherwise who could have given up before that daughter-in-law. The room has been allotted to me, and even now if I send a simple application the couple will be beaten to a pulp and taught a lesson.'

The wind began to strike against the boulders on the steppe. Jagarnath thought that the boulders were—self-oriented or selfish like him—waiting and wishing to see a split in the clouds and praying for rain that would cover them under water.

When Indravati saw Jagarnath getting up and going outside the tent, she got up slowly. She jumped over the blanket. She adjusted the pillow of Pupa. She wiped his forehead and turned him to the other side. She turned his face towards the cooler. When she came back, Kamla received a touch. As if she was woken up right then, she impulsively got up, 'Is it all right, Indra? Where did he go?'

Indra replied, 'Nothing. Sleep. I adjusted the pillow of Pupa. He becomes warm quickly. He sweats a lot. Boabji must have gone out.'

Kamla explained, 'I had just got sleep. God knows, I can't sleep tonight. I was very restive. I did not disturb you. I thought you will lose sleep. You were snoring a lot!'

Indra smiled, 'Who was snoring? You must have been dreaming. No one will hear the sound of my breathing let alone snores. Pupa's father

used to tell everyone how peacefully I slept.... Still, I don't know now....
May my life be sacrificed on you, sleep now!'

Kamla put her hand on Indra's mouth, 'Your enemies be sacrificed on
me! May the light and support of your son remain with you! You have
helped us when we were in great difficulty. You have suffered because
of us.'

Indra held Kamla's hand in her hands, 'Never say anything like this.
My life has become better because of your arrival. You should say that
you and we have done good deeds because of which we have been tied together under one tent. May my daughter Veena retain the luminous forehead! May she rule!!'

Kamla joined in, as if mixing her blessing with that of Indra, 'May good
nature and fortune descend on her!!'

The wind must have grown furious outside. There came the sound of
Jagarnath's footfall and both women disappeared inside their beddings.
Indravati wrapped herself in a sheet and Kamla began to snore. Jagarnath
got to the plank and stretched himself.

Indravati felt it was true that getting tied to Kamlavati was the fruit of
her good deeds but she was desperate to cut this connection. The mention
of the son-in-law made her blood burn because he was allowing his wife
to name the ration card in the name of her mother. She affirmed that she
would not hide anything now. I will tell categorically to Veena to make
a decision about me. After cutting the supplementary expenses, you
are sending paltry relief money. After what has happened, why are you
depriving me of my right?! Talk to your husband. Tell him that you are
now employed. The room is that of your father, for free and my widowed
mother is also after this money. On top of that my mother has to take care
of your mother and father. Has anyone seen days like these?! After all why
should my mother keep begging you?! Who are you?!

Kamla prayed for her daughter-in-law, Veena and wished her good.
According to her, the daughter-in-law did not have good intentions. She
tried to make her son's mother-in-law understand that it was the fault of
her son that he turned against his parents. However, Teja was way too raw
and naive. The daughter-in-law had worked magic on him. Now even the
relief amount had increased but he is giving them the same trivial sum.
The doctor has advised her to take a cup of milk every day, but how could
she do that? She could not fulfil her basic needs, let alone buy milk. They

did not get milk for the tea. Her stomach was all holes. What should she tell and to whom? At home in Kashmir, she had two milk-yielding cows. She felt scalded whenever she recalled her home.

Indravati's sleep had disappeared. Everyone was eager for rain but she was dying with the feeling that this time around the tent would not survive the rain. On top of that, she was telling Kamla, 'You suffered because of us.' 'Dear, if you are so worried about my suffering then why don't you get rid of me? I will live here as I deem fit. For us, mother and son, this tent is enough. The way I have spent the last eight years here, I shall spend the rest of my life,' she said to herself.

However, she knew that her daughter was bent upon giving her trouble. 'She is not transferring the ration card to my name. After getting her husband, a curtain has fallen on her eyes. She only takes care of her luxuries and is least bothered about her mother. I will send Pupa to her tomorrow morning. She will have to make a decision about me. How long can I keep the lie covered up!'

Jagarnath turned. He was waiting for a storm of a rain that would drive away all the tents. 'And when this Indravati begs me for help and protection, then she would find out who was dependent on whom. Despite being the father of a son, I feel high and dry.'

He said, 'I will go right now to the camp below and break my son's door into "my" room. He cannot stop me. The room has been allotted to me and is in my name. Let him come here with his wife. To his in-laws' tent and serve his mother and brother-in-law. This Indravati will also come down from her high pedestal.'

Indravati felt she was not covered and instinctively got up. Jagarnath asked, 'What happened?'

After adjusting her clothes, Indravati replied, 'I suddenly recalled I had not kept water bottle for you people. I saw you have perhaps woken up. I thought you were looking for water.'

Jagarnath lowered his eyes, 'You are making me feel ashamed. Don't worry. I should have moved and got the water bottle.'

Indravati got up rubbing her eyes and adjusting a part of the end of her dhoti on her head, 'I am ashamed myself. Your respect is priceless. May God shower you with honor! What have I done for you people? Nothing. I feel ashamed to keep you in this small tent. It would not have been a big deal if I had to rent a room for you people.'

It seemed Kamlavati had also woken up due to the ongoing conversation, 'My God! What else could you have done for us? Now we are tied to each other in joy and sorrow. And yet, you have not left anything undone for us.'

Apparently, Jagarnath was impressed, 'You are a goddess. Otherwise, we are witness to what is happening these days. Don't you see even God is not happy with us? The whole country received rain and here is not even a sign of the same.'

Internally, Indravati was lost in her thoughts. She was strengthening her determination made earlier. 'I will send Pupa across the rivulet early morning and will call Veena here. This Kamlavati is merely using me and thinking I'm from the daughter's side and will not throw them out. She is deluding herself.'

Kamlavati knew that Indra will not fall asleep easily. 'She must be thinking of strategy with her daughter, so that they can take us out of here.' Then she felt like telling her, 'Am I here of my own volition, in your tent? We have got our own *pucca*[1] room. It is because of the stratagem of your daughter that we are here. But not for long. Tomorrow itself I will ask my son to make a decision about us. Early morning I will send Pupa and call him here. But he is unable to decide for himself? Whatever his wife tells him he repeats like a parrot. And here is his father. He does not care a whit. He goes away in the morning and then after doing god knows what he returns in the evening. I have to spend twenty-four hours here with my son's in-laws. All misery is on my head.'

The wind had gathered speed. The conversations of the inhabitants of the steppe camp had also increased. It was not clear whether they were happy expecting rain or had become worried about the coming danger of the storm. Because of the wind pebbles were striking against the tent. All around there volumes of dust had gathered.

Pupa was fast asleep. All the other three people in the tent were pretending to be asleep. The rain started and in no time there was a heavy downpour. All people disappeared into the tents.

The tent began to sag. From beneath, the water began to enter inside. All four of them got onto the wooden plank and held bundles of clothes in their laps. The rain came down in sheets, and with each sheet

---

[1] Concrete.

of rain the ropes of the tent were pulled as if an earthquake had struck. The women began to pray, 'Om Namashivaai.' Jagarnath also panicked but was encouraging them. The lightning was sending the steppe colony topsy turvy. Indravati and Kamla had Pupa between themselves and continued to remain alive by looking at each other. Almost hugging each other. Jagarnath was making Pupa recite loudly with himself, 'Hear my prayers, O goddess! No one is there but you to take care of me!'

God knows when the rain had stopped and when dawn had come. All four of them were like a knot on the wooden plank. The leg of one was in the lap of another, and another's head was under the feet of yet another. Meanwhile, Indravati shrieked, 'Dear Pupa! What misery has caught me? Where is my Pupa?'

She began to beat her chest. Like a mystic, she came out bare-footed and uncovered hair. Following her came out Jagarnath and Kamla. The inhabitants of the camp were collecting the washed and flung out clothes, utensils, and the tents which had fallen. They heard about Pupa having gone missing. They stood up for a while but then who had time for that. Indravati got down wailing by the bank of the monsoon stream and then saw Pupa seated on a boulder. He was staring at the roaring and muddied water. She took him up and held him tight against her chest.

'My dear, I am deeply troubled! Where have you run away? Why did you have to come here? Thank God your foot did not slip or you would have fallen into the rivulet. Who knows when these dry streams will burst forth? God knows when a flood will descend and will sweep the unaware people off their feet. Take yesterday's rainstorm!'

Just then came Jagarnath and Kamlavati. Kamla also held Pupa in a tight embrace. 'Where had you gone? After all, where did you have to go? You nearly killed us!'

Pupa did not say anything.

Finally, Jagarnath encouraged him to speak. 'Why dear son, why are you not saying anything?'

After a short while Pupa sat down and keeping his head down, he said, 'I had been to my Deid, my sister. To the camp below.'

'To Deid's place? In this storm?' Kamla asked him surprised.

'What did you have to do there?' Indra asked him.

'Did you not think that the dry stream must be flooded? How could you have crossed?' Kamla said.

'I had come here walking to the bank. I had thought I would cross over the bridge. Then I would go down into the camp on the other side after walking over the bank across. Here I saw that even the bridge was washed away. Only a pile of stones was left behind on this side,' Pupa told them.

'But tell me what did you have to do there at this time? Did anyone tell you to go there?' Indra asked him.

Pupa remained silent. He only stealthily looked at Jagarnath. He also asked him, 'Yes, dear. What for did you want to go there?'

Now Pupa looked at Kamlavati. Jagarnath turned to his wife, 'Did you tell him anything, Kamla?'

'Curse on me if I have told him! Why should I have told him?' returned Kamla.

Jagarnath felt that his mother might have told him. He looked at Indravati.

Indravati thought, 'He is her son. Even if I have told him what do they have to do with that? ... But why should I allow them to suspect me?' The couple was looking at each other as if they had been accused of theft. Jagarnath was thinking, 'I am a close relative. I cannot nudge him further. But then his mother will suspect us. We are caught up and with that we will further regret our situation.' He thought that Pupa was a child and would speak out the truth if reprimanded.

'Pupa! Don't you know me? I will slap you and you will speak out everything! Say why and where you went, when there had been no light yet, and without asking anyone?' Jagarnath asked in with a stern voice.

Pupa was brimming with tears and he looked at Kamlavati. She felt her heart beating loudly and was wondering whether she had unwittingly told him. But then Pupa began to weep and told Jagarnath in a loud voice, 'Weren't you saying that early morning you would throw Teja out of the room? And we would complain about how on earth do they have two ration cards?'

'What! When did I say this? Whom did I tell this?' Jagarnath asked in surprise.

'Were you not talking to yourself about this? During the night when you came out of the tent and smoked a cigarette and then came back to sleep?' Pupa replied.

Indravati felt as if her heart had abruptly stopped beating. 'What? Did you say this? My God! My God! Were you saying this about your own son?'

Jagarnath had lost his sense and his balance when Pupa had said this. He summoned a lot of courage. 'What? Dear, you believe the words of a child? God knows what he has been dreaming about.'

In no time Kamla understood the consequences if Pupa's words were proved. She visualized a boat capsizing in the water. She quickly had an idea. She placed her hand on Pupa's head. 'My dear, beloved Pupa! You should not tell lies!'

Indravati caught hold of Pupa and held him against herself. 'So you had gone there to inform them beforehand? Are you so concerned about your sister and brother-in-law?'

Jagarnath was repeatedly swearing about his innocence. 'May death strike here and now to the person who said this! . . . Whom did I tell during the night? He was asleep. I went outside the tent because inside it was suffocating. But out there at midnight, to whom I could have said this?'

Kamlavati tried to control the situation. She smiled and turned to her husband. 'Now you are also behaving like this suckling child. How can any parents wish ill will and sorrow for their lone obedient son and agreeable daughter-in-law? We have of our own volition handed them the room which the government had given to us.' After saying this she turned her eyes towards Indravati to gauge her reaction.

Indravati had for the first time heard the word agreeable about her daughter from the mouth of Kamlavati. She also got a smile on her lips. 'Yes, that is right. Not all are lucky to get a gentle cow of a daughter-in-law like Veena. Having said that which couple does not wish to live separately from their parents?! We should only wish them the best of luck. Let us return to our tent. We should arrange food and drink.'

Jagarnath was casting side glances at Pupa and chewing his lips. 'I did not issue a whimper, how come he entered my mind?' And Pupa was looking at Kamlavati with rage, so much so that she was frightened. She wondered whether she had also said something which he had heard. She looked at Indravati with a smiling face.

Indravati was lost in her thoughts and was not sure about the truth. She was wondering about the same. 'Only God knows. Thank God, I did not myself die.'

Both the women had placed their hands on the shoulders of Pupa, and were walking alongside him. Jagarnath was looking behind and thanking God that the bridge had been taken away by the water.

Making sure that no one could hear, he called out to the roaring stream, 'Accursed one! You are better off when you are dry!' Then he scarily lifted his sight towards Pupa, to figure out whether he had heard anything.

10

Panj Tantra

(1997)

Abstract: *The story is that of a narrator and an imaginary listener. The narrator tells him about his wife who longs to go back to Kashmir after ten years in exile, to see the children playing under mulberry trees. Then he tells him how Thokar Chand got a helper for them in Jammu. The name of the helper was Bodhraj. Bodhraj later on, like the narrator's wife, longs to find his cow in Kistawar, his native place, and hand it to his friends Hassan and Obul. If Bodhrajj's desire to go back to his native home and find his white-spotted cow is futile, then how is the desire for a home in the narrator and his wife meaningful? The Listener calls the narrator's tale a Panj Tantra because there are five characters and five associate segments: narrator, wife, Thokar Chand, Bodhraj, and Hassan and Obul taken as one.*

Today he was again looking cross. Suddenly, out of nowhere, he popped up before me.

I asked him, 'Yes, can you share your problem with me?' 'Problem? I don't have any problem. Life these days is serious and convoluted. No story can describe it. No description is possible.'

'But I will share my story only with you. I will tell you what befell me.' I told him.

'What do I have to do with that? You just tell me the story of current life.' He said.

'What befell me is also a part of current life.' I responded.

'How?' He asked.

'Listen,' I began my story, 'Whenever—even today—the exit from Kashmir is mentioned my wife begins to shed tears. We cannot move out of our home for eight months in a year in Jammu. Heat exudes from walls and pillars and no one pauses on the way to ask for others' well-being.

Rupture. Rattan Lal Shant, Translated by Dr Javaid Iqbal Bhat, Oxford University Press. © Oxford University Press 2022. DOI: 10.1093/oso/9780192865083.003.0010

Elders and the young ones, all remain confined to their homes. And the small kids! Forget about them. The deathly silence also suffocates me, and my wife heaves long sighs.'

In Kashmir, even on hot days we used to go out in the courtyards, and, sitting under the mulberry trees, used to watch children of the mohalla play tip or cricket. Here in Jammu, she feels surprised that children no longer know how to play or to make those childish sounds. From inside her mind, she summons the sight of the mulberry tree of her courtyard and wonders about the past and the present. I can't tell you how many times she has asked me if only she could go there just once, only to see those frolicking children. I try to be logical with her and tell her that those children will not be children anymore. They must be grownups now. She refuses to be convinced. God knows if anyone at all even looks towards our desolate courtyard in Kashmir.

I read her aloud that news in which some leader had mentioned that the exiled Kashmiris would be brought back to their homes. But, heaving a sigh, she says, 'God knows how! Our roots are cut off. Our children have scattered in India and abroad for feeding themselves.... Just saying meaningless things, these people.... But those children in our courtyard! Where will they be? They will never forget us!'

'Today the same happened again. I read the news and she choked with tears. Providence interceded as if someone hurled Thokar Chand into our home.'

He broke into my talk, 'This is your habit. Quietly you brought in this Thokar Chand. First, you tell me, is this Thokar Chand important for the mental evolution of those two other characters or you brought him to prolong the story?'

I was surprised to hear this; amazed at the point he focused on. I told him, 'No, you see life does not revolve around just one or two characters. Other people will also come and develop some relationship with them. For the time being, you listen, you will get to know everything; I returned to the story.'

'To make the ambiance of my home light and happy I had a longer pre-liminary interaction with Thokar Chand. Along with him was a ten to eleven-year-old boy. He was wearing a dirty and torn shirt and ragged short pants. As if he had been told how to behave, he came down on my feet, as soon as he arrived.... "Namaskar Daddy!"' Then he went to my wife and said 'Namaskar Mummy!!'

'Pure Kishtawar accent. Kashmiri!

My wife wiped her tears and stared at him. I was also surprised about the identity of this person.'

I saw him become a little restless because after Thokar Chand I had brought Bodhraj into my story. To keep his interest in the story, I told him, 'I hope you will not ask anything. I do not wish to unnecessarily prolong it.... Listen.'

Thokar Chand narrated to us a long story about the boy. The gist was something like this. *This boy named Bodhraj was from a remote village in Doda and a relative of Thokar. Two years ago, he had told Bodhraj's parents that he will take him to Jammu and keep him with some person who would teach him to read and write and help him get a job when he becomes an adult. Otherwise, he would only wander among the steppes and forests and remain dull and dumb. Thokar had our home in mind. But Bodhraj's mother refused and the boy was addicted to roaming with friends.*

Then one night some gunmen appeared and they turned the whole village upside down. Bodhraj's father, uncle, and cousin were killed.

His mother was distraught. The whole village became deserted and she also left with her four children and went to her brother in Ramban. He was a waiter in some hotel. How many would he have taken care of? The mother began to find a way for herself. She handed over her elder son Bodhraj in the custody of Thokar Chand. Her second son was ten years old and she left him with some cycle repairman as an apprentice so that he would be able to eke out a living. She used to say that Bodhraj was mature and intelligent. By some unknown fortune, he came to me, the ill-fated one! She reminded Thokar Chand that he could take him to Jammu on the condition that he learned to read and write. He would then search for himself a livelihood.

We both became pensive after hearing the story of Bodhraj.

'Thank God the story of Bodhraj is over. Thank you for being brief. But Thokar Chand, who brought this boy to you, and with whom you said some relationship had been developed, who was he?' he asked me.

'Don't make haste. I told you earlier that is just one tale of my life. Every character and event have significance in it—both Thokar as well as Bodhraj,' I told him.

'But you are making a character out of character and incident from in-cident,' he said.

'The story is like that,' I returned.

'Okay now, be quick. Tell me about Thokar only that is important.'

'Absolutely. Not a bit more than that.' I assured him.

Thokar Chand had come to Kashmir either or ten years earlier in search of a job. In Kishtawar some leader had given him the promise of a job and asked him to come to Srinagar; however, he could not find him in Srinagar. The political middlemen gave him assurances but he could not get anything until the soles of his shoes wore off making rounds of their places. During this search, he somehow found a way to our home. He helped in domestic chores in the morning and evening; and spent the day carrying my applications from one office to the other. In this way, six to seven months passed and eventually, he became hopeless. Finally, he worked with one or the other shopkeeper on daily wages. He had a tenth examination pass, matriculation certificate. Although, according to him, he had got that after giving the superintendent of examinations a hen, corn cobs and a bag of beans, for which he was allowed to copy from the books.

I got him books and notebooks and began with the basics from the preliminary alphabet. He showed some interest and within a year was able to write an ordinary letter or an application. He managed to collect two or three hundred rupees and sent a money order to his home. In reply, he got his father's call to return. He went home and was married. He has got a child and now for the last three years is doing some work of his own in Jammu. He has not forgotten. He was saying, 'Sir, next year my child will be seven. Then I will hand him to you. You can bring him up the way you like.'

But my wife was not willing to keep the child of Thokar. 'We do not have space here,' she would say, 'We are shrunk in two small rented rooms. We do not know where we will be in the coming times!'

I agreed with what my wife was saying.

Today when this boy Bodhraj greeted me with Namaskaar, I felt as if he recited some mantra. She felt glad and I was speechless.

'Yes, yes, what did you have to do with Thokar now? Now Bodhraj is important. The selfishness of going about one's way, what else.' He hit an arrow of allegation, 'Hope Bodhraj does not now bring some other character with him, and then I have to suffer listening to his tale as well.'

I agreed with him that I should not bring anyone else but if events become like that.

The word 'events' alerted him (to the possibility of more stories). 'Hey, please don't stretch out these events. Can you tell me what you have to say through these above-mentioned events? Don't unnecessarily exaggerate the story!' he said in a tone of exasperation.

I tried to reason with him.

See my friend, a human being is not a motionless thinking statue. Due to his emotions and sentiments, he creates new relations with people, and sometimes they break also.... Listen.

Bodhraj mixed thoroughly in the affairs of our home. In a few days, he got familiar with the family as if he had been living here for years together.

In the morning I used to get ready to go to the market, and he would quickly, without notice, run to the milkman. Before I could reach there, he had milked the cow at milkman's home and collected about five liters of milk. The milkman also seemed to be kind to him or he was just using him. Bodhraj used to hold the bucket with greater verve than the milkman or his wife. Then he used to return with the milk from there.

He would get flowers on the way from the flower-selling woman and give them to my wife. She used to pray with Bodhraj sitting next to her until she had completed the puja.

Even before we had finished having tea, he would almost snatch the cups from our hands and wash them.... Going inside the kitchen, handing her water or sometimes the vessels ... putting a cup or two of rice in a plate and sifting it in no time. When I was reading or writing he used to sit seriously in front of me, turning the pages of the book and trying to identify something.

Early morning Bodhraj used to bring the newspaper for me. This was a work of special interest for him. When I had finished reading the newspaper, he would ask whether there was any news of his village in the paper. This used to worry me because it was a signal that he had not forgotten the tragedy at home. On many occasions, I would change the topic and forbade him from bringing the newspaper because the newspaper refreshed his memory. Otherwise, the childish things he did would make him forget about anything else.

One day I was reading the newspaper, and he broke in to say, 'Daddy! Is there a mention of Hasna or Obla in the newspaper?'

I replied, 'No.' After four or five days he again asked the question. This time I was a little annoyed, 'Why are you pestering? God knows, where are they? Why should their names be written here?'

I noticed that he would later in the day, long after I had read the newspaper, take the newspaper to my wife, and ask for the names of people whose photos were published.

Seven or eight months passed. Bodhraj had become a part of the family. Twice Mummy ji had sewn his shirt and pants. I bought him a pair of shoes. He used to wear a nylon slipper. He had preserved his shoes and pants. Sometimes when I would give him ten or twenty rupees or a rupee or two, he would keep them with Mummy ji. Then he would forget how much he had kept with her. She would put some more money on that and buy him some clothes or other items which would make him happy. He had almost forgotten his brothers and his mother. He never spoke about them. Whenever I gave him any work to do like writing or memorising a lesson or learning the mathematical tables, he would do that quickly. I admitted him to a nearby primary school. He made friends there in no time who sometimes came to our home in the evening to play with him.

He tried to get up and leave. I got his drift and told him, 'Listen, the story's last and most important part is yet to come. In this is Hasna and Obul—the central characters.'

'I heard. Central characters!! Up to now was Bodhraj, before him Thokar Chand and even before him you and your wife…. After all, when will the sequence wind up? …. What are you up to? What do you want to say?' he asked with obvious irritation.

'I am only telling you about my afflictions.'

'Is it still your story?' he said in a matter of fact tone.

'But I was the one reading the newspaper!!' I smiled and he joined in.

'Now you are trying to crack jokes,' he said.

'No dear, the reality is that this story is actually of Hasna and Obul,' I returned to him.

'How is that so?' he asked.

Listen.

'One day the newspapers had published pictures of some children. On that day Bodhraj brought the newspaper before me. I was waiting for him to ask whether anyone among these children was Hasna or Obul. But perhaps he feared I might scold him for asking or he had himself searched for them and not found anyone.'

I asked him, 'Why are you so speechless? Do you want to ask anything?'

He kept looking at me with the eyes of a ram. Then he answered in a half-voice, 'Daddy, you do not know about Hasna and Obul. They must be missing me a lot!'

I felt that Bodhraj was feeling very irritated. I replied 'Maybe. But what can one do.'

Another month passed by. One day I was writing a letter. Bodhraj came with a notebook and pen so that he could write a letter to a relative who was working as a *Chaprasi*[1] in Kishtawar. I had to almost hold his hand to write a letter. He wrote in the letter—*Go to my village. Search for my white-spotted cow. After finding it, hand it to Hassan and tell him to take care of her along with his own and take her to the forest (for grazing).*

I thought I would tell him, 'How can your cow be found after one year. Even if they found it with someone, will he give it back?' But I did not tell him anything.

And he also wrote that his corn cobs must be ready. *Take out the cobs and send them to my mother at Ramban.*

One day my wife asked me, 'Has Thokar Chand asked you about the salary of Bodhraj?'

Salary? I was surprised. This boy had spent over a year in our house yet there had been no mention of the salary. The salary was not mentioned by Thokar Chand in Kashmir or even asked for it. I would forcefully put five, eight hundred rupees in his pocket when he used to go to Kishtwar which he accepted with great difficulty, saying, 'I am doing my work here

---

[1] An orderly.

and looking for a job. I am eating and drinking in your family. You don't owe me any money.' On his return, he used to bring beans, soya, corn cobs from his village and placed them before us. He was an egotist, not receiving money easily and yet giving us a lot of things.

Bodhraj was also no less an egotist. Even if he got some money from prizes, etc., he would not keep an account of it. My wife reminded him at the time of buying things that he had collected this much of money.

One day it seemed that he was missing his village. I asked him, 'Do you wish to meet your mother at Ramban?'

He did not respond and left.

My wife told me one day, 'He has collected more money than he could have through salaries. But that is different. You should have asked Thokar how much we should give him. Maybe he is expecting more money. Here it is difficult to pay even the house rent. We hardly manage to fill our bellies in this alien land. Wherefrom will I bring seven hundred and fifty rupees for him? He does not touch the money he has collected. Maybe he feels he wants a separate amount. Perhaps he is asking for a salary.'

To decide about the salary of Bodhraj I called Thokar Chand. When he heard about the salary Thokar told Bodhraj, 'Seven hundred and fifty! Dear, you are lucky that you are living with them. They are taking more care of you than they would of their own child. . . . They will teach you, make you write so that you get a job when you grow up. After all what do you have to do with the money? Do you have to give it to your mother?'

Bodhraj was quietly listening and Thokar seemed to be regretful as if it was his fault. Finally, the obstinacy of the boy opened my mind and I began to reflect. I thought if this boy asked for a salary, he did not commit any wrong. I did not see anything surprising in this. And I prepared him for departure to Ramban. Thokar would accompany him. But now Bodhraj broke his silence. He feigned excuses. It seemed, suddenly, all tragedy had descended on him. He was insisting on us that his mother must not be informed that he was going to the village.

I tried to make him understand that he had left the village three years ago, we did not know the present condition there. From newspapers only we got to know how much the situation had changed. 'God knows whether your white-spotted cow will be there or not. Where and how will you find it there? Do we know the state of your land and other property? Your village was deserted on that very day.'

His answer made me speechless. 'You were reading in the newspaper that one big leader has said that all of us have to go back home in Kashmir.'

I again tried to make him understand, 'This is what leaders say. Those who made you leave, unless they say, we can't go back to Kashmir.' He did not understand this. Then he told me very innocently, 'Daddy, I want to go straight to the house of Obula and Hassan. I will hand them the custody of my white-spotted cow and return. And I will give them five hundred rupees to look after my cow.' 'But Hassan and Obula will be god knows where! Who knows whether they will even be cowherds now?' I replied.

Bodhraj sat gazing at me. I felt he did not understand what I was saying.

My wife was watching with great restiveness, wondering what might happen now. But I recalled that time when Bodhraj had not yet come to our home and my wife also had not understood that the children who were playing in our courtyard in Kashmir might have become old now and God knows where they will be. Since then ten years have passed.

'We passed that night in great pain. The next day Bodhraj again got busy with the routine of the home.'

'Please stop. I have understood it now ... You name it Panj Tantra,' he said very coolly as if he had found a solution to some problem.

'I am not saying this just because like Panj Tantra a story emerges out of a story and a character comes out of a character but also because like the former it has five separate characters,' he told me. 'See, you and your wife make two, with Thokar and Bodhraj there are four. Hasna and Obul together make the fifth.'

I knew that he was an irksome fellow. But his interpretation in this manner and providing the example of Panj Tantra put me off my rocker. I too began to count something. I informed him, 'Hasna and Obul are two distinct characters.'

'But their role is similar, and we don't know what it is like. They are symbols,' he said. Hearing the word 'symbol' made me realize that my whole endeavour to tell him the story had gone waste.

He felt my apprehension and said, 'What if we consider the whole Panj Tantra also symbolic. Listen, if it is a symbol then we have heard better stories than yours. Five branches, five characters, Panj Tantra!' Saying this he left, without much notice. The same way as he had come.

He could hardly bear anyone when it came to his knowledge and understanding, and on my part, I was not able to figure out the number of characters. Am I and my wife two separate characters, and Hasna and Obul just one!!!

11

Intervention

(2000)

Abstract: *The third-person narrator tells the reader that Autar Krishan has returned to Jammu after seven years from Kashmir. His mother-in-law Kamlavati has died. The other Hindu migrants in the refugee camp are angry at his arrival. Because he had abandoned his wife Usha and daughter Pinky with his mother-in-law Kamlavati in Jammu. They suspect that he has come to light the pyre and he will slip back to Kashmir leaving behind his wife and daughter. However, dead Kamlavati, surprisingly, does not close her mouth until her son-in-law, daughter, and granddaughter have put water in her mouth. The refugee camp dwellers find out to their utter surprise that Autar has returned to Jammu for good.*

Please listen to the whole story first. Then you should decide whether we interfere in the private lives of others or not. Although, if there had not been an atmosphere of mourning, we would have beaten Autar black and blue, and then told him why he was beaten.

Autar was not regretting his bad deeds. When he came, out of humanitarian considerations two boys held his two trunks and bedding, etc. They helped him take off his coat and pants, and in putting on his shirt and trousers so that he could sit for the last rituals. His lack of regret showed in a couple of things which he said for which time and place were not appropriate. 'Do not show sympathy towards me here,' he said 'I know everything. How in the last seven years my relatives and other people here were backbiting against me and saying:

'Hey, Autar is finished. He has changed his *varna*[1] in Kashmir. It is said that he has also changed his name. He is very close to militants.

---

[1] Caste, class. There are four varnas in Hinduism: Brahmins, Kshatriyas, Vaishyas, and Shudras.

Rupture. Rattan Lal Shant, Translated by Dr Javaid Iqbal Bhat, Oxford University Press. © Oxford University Press 2022. DOI: 10.1093/oso/9780192865083.003.0011

He merrily goes to his office in the village every day. He lives in some neighbour's house. He has left his wife. He has sunk into some pit.' He quoted what they were saying about him in his absence.

I told you that the time was not appropriate. Otherwise, he had to account for a lot of things and would have said each and every thing, which we would have asked. Right now, the dead body of Kamlavati was waiting since morning for someone to set it alight. In autumn it does not take long for the day to end.

When at midnight we heard that she had breathed her last, right then all the people assembled. Our worry was who would perform her last rites and set the pyre alight.

Kamlavati had just one relative, Usha, and she was staying with her. Usha was not weeping nor did she scream, as we might have apprehended but remained holding onto the body of Kamlavati.

Kamlavati had one sister who was living in Bangalore with her son. She was also informed but it would take her three to four days to reach here.

This became a big problem for us. Meanwhile, someone said, or recalled, that she has a son-in-law in Kashmir who she regarded as her son, and had brought home as a resident son-in-law. The problem had to be resolved with the consultation of Usha but she was speechless, in a tight embrace with her mother's body. Neither saying anything nor answering any question. Her ten-year-old daughter Pinky sometimes looked at her mother and sometimes at the lifeless face of her grandmother.

Time was running out. With great difficulty we were able to send information to Autar Krishan in Kashmir, although hardly anyone had any contact with him. Usha herself had no information, let alone others.

But his arrival and presence became a problem for the whole camp. We thought Autar would come and perform the last rites of his mother-in-law, and that would be good. And if he does not come, one among us will do that. For she used to call us her sons. For the last three years, Kamlavati's sickness kept getting worse, and we used to assist her. We gave her the last sips of water. Because Usha had no one else with her here.

Usha became very obstinate. We tried a lot to take her away from the body but she dragged the latter with her. Then we left that and began to make other arrangements. We did not have much hope of Autar's arrival.

But he arrived! It was a little later in the afternoon. We went to sympathize with him and assist him but he frowned on us, saying, 'Don't show me sympathy.'

About four years ago, when Usha fell so ill that we did not know whether she would survive, information was sent to her husband but he did not come. Usha had given up hope and used to say, 'With what face will he come here? I had come to know that very day when he drove us to Jammu and stayed there himself. Khaleel had lured him to riches and prosperity in those very turbulent days, and they began to do business. God knows what! He lost whatever he had; with the greed of earning a lot, he did not leave Kashmir. After that, it never crossed his mind what I as a widow must be doing here along with my widowed mother and a lone daughter.... But for the aid of my Bhagwaan and the pains which my brothers and sisters took upon themselves in the Camp, I would neither have got this room nor would have this relief-money been coming in.'

Usha used to confess this to all but we stopped her from doing this, for reasons of faith and mercy. Whatever we heard about her or her husband's relatives was from her own mouth. We never nudged her to say anything. But we used to see how her eyes became red and her body shivered while saying all these things. It appeared she had to say more and spit venom against her husband. Then we used to change the topic of the conversation.

Then finally when Autar Krishan arrived after seven years, that too at the death of his mother-in-law, the whole affair became suspicious. He came and changed into a *kurta pajama*[2] and sat down for the last rites. He neither went to drop water into Kamlavati's mouth nor to see her face for the last time, nor did he go to console his wife. At least he could have talked with his daughter. Because of his arrival in this manner and then due to his peculiar behaviour, the atmosphere had become serious. Everyone was feeling angry with him. He must have also felt it. While doing the last rituals, he began to speak, 'Ten times I sent her messages to come to Kashmir. Everything is fine there now. Come and see for yourself. I go every day to the village for work. I have got more respect than before. I earn more money than before. So many officers came and went, and no one dares touch me. What could they have done to me? I was doing for

---

[2] Shirt and trouser.

them things that no one else could lay hands on. Sometimes even going to the office on holidays. And then, what did I have to do at home!'

Autar was busy doing the funeral rites but it was clear that he was explaining himself to appear good before us. 'Her mother was poisoning her ears against me. It was she who drove her out from there,' he continued.

I hope you do not believe that we were getting impressed by what he was saying. But we believed that he was trying to cover his ill deeds and trying to get the sympathy of the strangers who had come to mourn the death. We were surprised to see that his *yoni* was also torn. Maybe he had bought it on the way to Jammu, otherwise what use was it to him in Kashmir.

We were looking forward to lifting the dead body before Usha herself became a dead body. That would be a tragedy. Leave him, he came today here because of the fear of what people will say of him. With evening he will slip away. He does not care for anyone. That was a general perception. We were not paying attention to his nonsense.

We all left behind everything in Kashmir, our homes and everything. But no one left behind a family member. When Usha came back after three years with her daughter, we tried hard to get her connected to her home. We had told her if her mother was the source of discord, she should leave her here to our care and go to Kashmir. 'The way you lived with him with a heavy heart and patience for three years, with the same manner you continue to stay and live with the husband.'

She would reply, 'When every one of us has lost his home there, what kind of business has he found there? These are all excuses. What has my mother done to him? Was it her fault that she handed him her orchard, land and the rest of the trees to him? She had told him—*you are my son and you will be my life-vest*.... And this is what he gave her in return. For the last eight years, this man has not even asked about her.... He did not even think that his daughter might have grown up. How on earth can I take her to Kashmir?'

After finishing the rites Autar got up and went far away to sit on a big stone, and lit up a cigarette. Some women came up and began to bathe Kamlavati. Autar did not even look towards that. His eyes had become lead. He got up from the stone, walked around, and then returned to his seating place. We did not have time at that moment to see his restlessness and listen to his pain. We got busy with making the Arthi. After a while, the collective prayer for the dead began.

Goram Har Mam Narak Ripo
Keshav Kalmash Bharam

Our eyes were set on him. He did not come close to the coffin. Although at that time all kinds of people came from the refugee camp, even those who had come to visit people, even those who were passing by. They came and began to pray to God, 'You are the One to release from hell, on me also have mercy O, God!'

Autar was feeling somewhat restless. At this time a man passed by him. He caught hold of him and began to tell him, 'Listen. I will tell you all, realistically. This, my wife, was adoring her mother. Now she has made her daughter the same. Her mother's sisters and their husbands had come to Jammu and they had incited her to come to Jammu. They left Jammu and reached Bangalore and left her here in the refugee camp.'

That man did not know the background. He asked him, 'But now you have come here to lit the pyre. That is good. Forget about the past now.'

At this, he almost pounced on him, 'No, that is not the issue. I did not know that here you people will speculate like that and tomorrow it will be the talk of the town.' Autar was shaking his head and denying the assumption that he had come just to light the pyre. Then he told him the reason for he felt that there is no way out. 'I received the information in the morning from the people around my home in Kashmir and I decided to leave for Jammu.'

Now it was natural that this man would ask him more. The issue had now become more mysterious. Actually, all the camp people had felt the same as the man. Otherwise, who had the time to search and evaluate the private life of Usha or that of her husband? But if someone starts to unravel himself, then it becomes necessary to listen to it and then after listening, to reflect on it. Here in Jammu, with so many migrant camps, no other camp had as much unity as our own.

Anyway, the man became worried after hearing Autar's response and asked him 'Why were you compelled to leave suddenly? Did you have any official work here? Have you been transferred here?'

'They care a lot about me. How can they transfer me! The day before yesterday was Sunday. He had told me to come to the office for the record had to be set straight for the departmental Inspection. There used to be hartal after hartal due to which we were not able to reach the office.... On that day in the evening when I reached the rented place, I saw there was a huge commotion. Khaleel had been injured and he had been taken to the hospital. All of them told me that the gunmen were looking for me and when they could not see me, they shot Khaleel in the arm and ran away.'

'But why had they come for you? Were you not known to them?' the man asked him.

"That is why I am also astonished.... I feel they had some misunderstanding ... I apprehended this one day when a colleague asked me in the office why I was reading my newspaper loudly in the bus. 'Why do you have to read aloud and make others listen?' "

'So what, this is an insignificant incident. Because of this they would not have come to kill you,' the man told him.

'Yes, this is their misunderstanding. I will resolve it with them. But right now the time was not appropriate for that. They also had the misconception that I have relatives in Jammu and that I do visit them,' Autar responded.

Kamlavati was being given a bath, and we could see and feel from the distance that Autar must be telling this stranger all kinds of brainless things. He might have come because of fear of some bad omen or felt that he would get the curse of the departed soul. He would come up to the cremation ground, lit her pyre, and then fly away. We decided we would not allow him to run away. We would bring him back and call him to account for abandoning his wife and his daughter. We would take revenge, there was no question of letting him go back to Kashmir.

Right then a problem arose. Usha was not letting go off the dead body. She clung to her mother's feet. We tried everything possible on her. Nothing worked. She became unconscious and swiftly fell to the ground.

What would we do? On the one hand, it was already evening. Some people got busy fanning her body and some in putting water in her mouth.

We were not able to do anything and then suddenly a miracle happened!

We saw Autar Krishan and the other man come; the same man to whom he was until now relating his legend (and this man later told us the whole story). Within no time Autar put his arms around her and lifted her away. He told us to pick up the dead body and go. He went inside along with Usha and Pinky.

We took the dead body quickly and our knees were almost frozen. Our minds are sinful; it is home to so many intrigues and desires. Somehow, we left, saying, 'Shau Shambu Apradha' but very slowly as if saying to ourselves. No one was saying anything. Meanwhile, someone broke in 'Hey, bring Autar! We can't trust him.' But we were walking forward.

We left the precincts of the camp but all of us were occasionally looking behind over our shoulders. All of a sudden, we stopped in.

At the time when the sun was setting on that autumn day, we saw Autar coming out of the room and walking towards us. On the one side he was holding Usha who had placed all her weight on Autar and was walking, step by step. They reached close to us. We kept the coffin down. Autar, Usha, and Pinki put water into the mouth of Kamlavati. The latter's mouth was also open up to this time, now it closed.

When we returned from the Ghat we found out that Autar had come with all his belongings from Kashmir. How could he go back?!!

And then 'we' had a peaceful sleep; 'We', the dwellers of this camp, those about whom you say that they interfere in the private lives of others.

12

Gauri's Div Gaam

(2005)

Abstract: *Gauri Shauri is from a village in Kashmir called Div Gaam, but now living in a refugee camp in Jammu. She fled from Kashmir with two precious things in a trunk: her husband's passbook and a blue cylindrical stone which is her deity, her Thokuir or Div Shuir. She desires to build a temple in the refugee camp and install this deity. Initially, the Camp dwellers are indifferent, and even her daughter-in-law Sheela is cynical and does not like her husband Pushkar going along with his mother with the planned construction of a temple. All along the story, Gauri recalls her life in the native village of Div Gaam from the day when she had come as a bride.*

1

'No, no . . . Don't tear away the flower.'

As soon as Gauri Shauri heard this shout from behind, she held her hand back.

The light of the dawn had started to appear on the horizon. There was no one visible for a long distance on either the left or the right. She lifted her gaze a little. She could not see anyone who made the shout. But as a person who appeared to be the owner of the house came before her, wearing only an undershirt and underwear, she turned her face away. Sweat broke out from her, and with her downcast face, she began to walk away with difficulty. Her legs grew heavy. She was caught stealing.

The owner of the house spoke to her again in a gentle tone as if he felt some pity for her, 'Why are you carrying away these flowers, *Mataji*?'[1]

---

[1] Mother.

Rupture. Rattan Lal Shant, Translated by Dr Javaid Iqbal Bhat, Oxford University Press. © Oxford University Press 2022. DOI: 10.1093/oso/9780192865083.003.0012

Her feet stopped in their way. She felt a hint of an allegation in this question which she was not willing to accept. Keeping her eyes down, she replied in a broken voice (attempting to speak in Urdu as the owner had questioned), 'These flowers ... for temple ... you will also receive blessings ... my son also along.' There was some clarity now and the seriousness of the scene came down. And when this man began to laugh aloud, Gauri Shauri felt embarrassed, wondering what she had told him.

'What did you say?' the owner asked, 'You are taking it to temple? When did I say you are taking it to eat? ... But, Mataji, where is the temple?'

His laughter and his last sentence rang in her ears until she reached the bank of a rivulet and sat on a big stone. From there the house was not visible from whose flower bed in a wall-less courtyard she had torn some flowers a few days ago; nor the well-built man in underwear and undershirt. Even then she felt like a thief in this forlorn place. Her eyes began to brim with tears. She reprimanded herself for coming by that way. 'Had I taken a different path my heart would not have been tempted by the flowers. This owner might have been lurking there for me, thinking that this *Battin*[2] is furtively stealing flowers. *Today I will catch her* ... He shouted at me like that ... O God! I wish the earth had opened up and swallowed me.'

Holding her forehead with her hand, she began to lament. 'He will indeed tell Pushkar Nath. Or he will come himself and start an argument. The whole camp of Pandits will fall upon me.'

She looked at herself. Her foot had strayed and felt cramped. Yesterday, her *dhoti* got entangled in a bush and snicked. 'What has happened to me, after all?' She got very angry with herself and said. '*Bhagwaan*[3] is and He is yours. Why are you decorating and persuading Him with stolen flowers?'

A few drops fell from her eye and seeped into the flowers in her hand. She thought, 'What is the fault of these flowers? It is good I can use them for Bhagwaan only after washing them with my tears. These are the last flowers. If you want to accept them, fine, from tomorrow you will not get even one petal.'

---

[2] Often used for Kashmiri Hindu women.
[3] God.

She got up without seeking anyone's help and encouraged herself. She put up the flowers on the long and rounded blue-coloured pestle which was against a boulder. There were thread-like white lines around the pestle. She folded her hands before it and without looking behind she began to walk fast. She heard the loud laughter and shout echoing all around her and running after her: 'But where is the temple?!!!'

She took a different path on the way back. Instead of walking on the bank, she walked through the rivulet. There were red and murky boulders on the right and the left as far as she could see, sun-baked stepping stones, as if this river had become spellbound. She felt that very soon a torrent of water would come and sweep away this blue cylindrical boulder of a foreign race, the one from Kashmir.

There was another hour before the sun would rise, but the light was enough to make the surroundings visible. Gauri was not sure where she had reached. There was no tree or living creature on the bank of the rivulet nor was any house visible from down there. She felt dizzy. Looking towards the rising sun, she folded her hands. 'Bhagwaan! Forgive my sins. Give the fruit of the flowers I have bedecked you with to the owner of these flowers. Which sin has he, poor one, committed? You had to rest at Div Gaam and I brought you here. There the Chinars gave you cool shade from all sides. Here you have to stay like this against a boulder for, who knows how long, feeling this heat and longing for the cool shade. Here you've no trees to give you shade. There you used to hear the music of the river the whole year; here you will get that only during *vaehraath*.[4] For a couple of days the water will smash your head against the bed until the water will carry the banks along. If you wish to punish anyone, do that to me. I am in a quandary and have put you in the same.... But show me the path of goodness now.'

She did not know how long she had been talking to herself, with the stony rivulet and sometimes with the sun god.

When she reached home, she sat for a short while on the bedstead near the door threshold. Sitting there she knocked on the door. Pushkar Nath woke up and opened the door. Rubbing his eyes, he came out, 'What is it?'

Asking him to sit on the bedstead, she told him in a low voice.

---

[4] The rainy season.

'Go to the post office today, dear. You had told me to wait for another year. Now, go and take a look. Tell me how much is ready.'

Pushkar Nath did not understand what determination had arisen in Mataji that she woke me up so early.

'And also raise the border around the plot of land by a foot or two to make a barrier.' She told him.

Looking far ahead into the distance, she was saying as if the hearer was her own self but slowly so that only Pushkar would listen. 'Then we will fill it with some soil and we will plant flowers around.' Pushkar asked why they needed to raise a barrier around the slope as if someone would take away the land. For a long distance no one owned land there so there was no chance of anybody grabbing it. And there was no chance that in the coming fifty years anyone from the village would come close to their land while constructing houses. 'Just for a few flower plants why should we spend money?' Don't know what hurry is driving Mataji.

But the colour of his mother's face had changed. Looking at her face he did not dare to say or ask anything. He felt the noise of Div Gaam in Kashmir might have struck against her again in her dream. 'Actually, she must be feeling homesick about the village.' He got up, stretched himself, and told her, 'Post office will open at 10 am.'

Gauri Shauri was restless. She picked her bedding, folded the bedstead, and took both inside the room where her daughter-in-law was still asleep.

Pushkar Nath realized that Mataji was restless. It was not just because of the dream. No one had yet arrived at the water tank. He went to the tap and washed his face, and returned to his mother who had by now mopped the door threshold and was seated there.

'Mataji, I forgot to tell you yesterday. Bittuji has sent five thousand rupees. He has written that in the temple yard three, four flower plants should be grown so that Mataji can get enough flowers for Bhagwaan.'

Hearing this Gauri Shauri's eyes welled up with tears.

'May my life be dedicated to him! He knows that his grandmother is mad after the flowers.... May my life be sacrificed on him and his ways! May Bhagwaan assist him wherever he is!'

Pushkar Nath said further, 'He has written that they will collect more money from Kashmiris there and send.'

'Yes, we better use that. May you never be short of anything you need, Bitta! .... Whatever you lay your hands on, wish it turns into a treasure.'

Gauri grew agile. As if the construction of the temple was withheld because of these five thousand rupees. She got up. She got the dhoti, and began to sew with a needle where it had snicked. Pushkar felt good that he had not given her the news yesterday although it did not go down well with Sheela. Because of his distaste of Sheela in this matter, he wanted to tell her the same time so that Sheela could feel the pinch.

'First of all, we will get the road to the temple opened up. The MLA has said that we should now apply for electricity.'

Right then Gauri remembered something. She stopped while needling through the dhoti and began to think about something. 'Natha, I don't know whether we did the right thing in buying this piece of land there ... Hope we did not make a mistake ... Who knows when the rivulet will overflow and take away all with it.'

'Don't nurse these unnecessary apprehensions. Neither it will be eroded nor will anyone steal it.'

There was silence for a moment. Pushkar sat on the door threshold to shave and his mother resumed sewing. Finally, she said to him, as if clearing the doubt about the incident which had happened earlier in the day so that owner of the house does not hurl any other accusation, 'That yellow coloured house. Which you said is that of the Sarpanch of that village. Which has barbed wire around his house ... and has big white flower plants. Did you locate it? There is no other house on the way from the camp to the temple.' Now Pushkar understood what she was referring to.

'Yes, recognised him. Saayein Das. What about him?'

'Nothing. Was just asking.'

'What can one say about him! Bhagwaan has been kind to him. He has a brick kiln and flour machine. He owns the village ... I don't know how he does not own our piece of land because he owns a lot of land here ... Not land, just these boulders and stones. Initially, all of Jammu was like this, made of rivulets and stones. One day a similar community will also emerge in our area. After all, why did Bhagwaan throw us on this side.'

Gauri Shauri was thinking about something. Meanwhile, Pushkar Nath continued, 'He is a friend ... Why did you mention him?'

She caught her tongue between her teeth. 'Nothing, just like that ... You should do what I told you to do.'

She got up after saying this. She had seen Sheela coming out and standing behind her. Pursing her lips, she told her,

'I had forgotten to mop the entrance to the home.'

Sheela had heard the secret conversation between mother and son. She had also heard that her mother-in-law did not want any neighbour to know. Therefore, discussions about land and noise of Div Gaam in Gauri's dreams were always conducted in whispers. That is why her mother-in-law turned to something else.

Sheela gave enough hints to her husband that she knew what was going on between mother and son. She said to him, 'Today you shaved early in the morning. Are you going anywhere else other than the post office?' She went back inside without hearing the answer.

The narrow ten-feet rooms of the camp had common walls and the tap of the tank was also common. It was natural that a person's secret would quickly do the rounds of the entire camp. More so in the case of Gauri Shauri and Pushkar Nath who had conversed outside the room, on the steps of the door threshold.

Gauri Shauri was not surprised when the daughter-in-law raised the matter while having tea. From the tenor of Sheela, Gauri Shauri could discern the mode of thought among the other residents of the camp. Sheela told her in a mild tone, giving the perception of closeness, 'Mataji, these Dogra villagers will one day make a temple somewhere, then you should also go there.'

Gauri Shauri raised her gaze towards her. 'Why is she asking such a question? She knows everything.' But she had yet to complete herself when Sheela said. 'You are unnecessarily wasting your money on useless places … After all, we have to live in this world … don't we have our expenses to meet?'

Pushkar Nath stole a look at his wife but she looked the other way.

Gauri Shauri knew why Sheela was talking about expenses today. Until yesterday she used to be up from bed before my arrival. Though Gauri would never let her do it Sheela asked her whether she should make tea for her. Today it appears she has changed. What happened during the night?! Gauri replied:

'May my life be sacrificed for Bittuji! May this Bhagwaan curse me, if I ever mentioned the temple before him! Or if I have ever asked him about money.'

Pushkar Nath felt Sheela was unnecessarily forcing mother-in-law to use swear words. He told her, 'Sheela, how much of an amount do you think five thousand rupees is? Besides, out of this, he has collected some from other Kashmiris. Even if he sends money what is the big deal? Ever since he has gone, he has not sent a penny. Tell this also to your friends with whom you sit gossiping. Don't just show off before them.'

His mother understood that her son was alluding to something regarding his conversation with his wife. She wondered what was being hinted at in his answer.

Sheela felt silent. After a while, she said, as if clarifying, 'I thought he has not been on the new post at Indore even for six months. He was saying that he might be sent to Madras. First setting up home at Indore and then Madras. I was thinking he might need money from us.'

Gauri Shauri was feeling that it might be wrong on her part to accept this money. But returning the money was not proper too. She told her with good wishes.

'This *Thokuir* god is with him everywhere.[5] With him and his family. Wherever he will go, he will protect him.'

Pushkar Nath felt that he should again say something, 'Sheela, no one becomes a pauper by spending five thousand rupees. And these have been collected from others as well.'

'Collected!' Gauri Shauri was startled but did not feel it appropriate to speak anymore on the matter. Pushkar Nath said, 'In the inner part of the city, Kashmiris had collected some donation. First, they had decided to construct a temple and name it Ganpat Yar. But they found later that the plan was not feasible.'

His wife cast a glance at him but ignoring that he got up and changed his clothes. He told his mother, 'I have to also meet the Patwari. He was saying there is an extra half-a-canal on the rivulet side. That has a common ownership of the people.'

Gauri Shauri did not understand. But she reminded him of something, 'You were saying that you would make arrangements for bricks and stones. Don't forget to speak to the person who will get the soil.'

'Did I not tell you that only a signal from Sayein Dass is enough, then all of it will be there.... Mataji, how sad that despite possessing all the

---

[5] Thokuir also means deity.

land around, this plot of land did not belong to him. Had it been so we would have got it for a few pennies. And is it possible that the temple would not have been constructed?'

'Yes, they're brimming with faith.'

'When they hear the name of the temple, all the villagers will come with enthusiasm. Just that the work should get started,' he said to his mother.

Sheela got an opportunity to speak. 'That is what I was telling you. They will construct a temple on their own. They will not need us.... You consult anyone in the camp. They will tell you the same thing.'

'Why do I need to do that? You are there every day consulting with them,' said Pushkar Nath getting up and casting a side glance at her.

He was reflecting on the way. 'Don't I know what kind of conversations go on among the people of the camp about us? Since we have taken this step of constructing a temple, has anyone even had the courtesy to ask us about the progress of our plan, let alone give any assistance?'

Gauri Shauri did not want the issue of the temple should lead to any ill will between her son and his wife. After Pushkar had left she got the greens along with their stems in a basket close to her and began to remove the stems from the greens. Taking off the skin of the stems and removing the green leaves, she mildly turned towards Sheela, 'Sheela, what did you feel, that Bitta sent money and I received that! I wish that I could take off my skin and put it on him. How can I bear if he remains there in need of money? For what do I need money? For the temple, just two rooms have to be put up, one for worship and the other smaller one for the Sadhu who will stay there. Do you know I have preserved the money of my late heaven-bound husband along with my own pension money which I have preserved for the same for the last four years? How much more do I need?!'

Sheela heard what she wanted to hear from her mother-in-law, and got up to the other corner of the room where on a table was the gas stove. She lit it with a matchstick and said with a smile, as if she was addressing her husband, 'You were and will remain your mother's son! You may not pay heed to what I tell you but I have taken a promise from your mother that the money of my son is in your custody.'

2

The laughter and the disdain of Sayein Das continued to pierce Gauri Shauri's mind ever since he had found her stealing the flowers that early morning. She did not dare to tell Pushkar Nath because he had told her that Sayein Das was a good human being, and for constructing the temple he can be very handy in many ways. Now she prayed to Bhagwaan that she should not meet him again and he should not come to know that she is Pushkar Nath's mother.

She stopped taking that route although that was the shortest. From the camp, on the bank of the rivulet, was a narrow half-a-mile path that led down to the big road. On one side of the path was the new house of Sayein Das. Behind his house, he had made a wide and concrete lane which went all the way into the village. But that lane ended on this narrow path. If this house had not been on the path and if she did not have a look at the blossoming white flowers while going and coming, maybe she would not have been tempted.

On that day she felt very sorry for her mistake and leaving that path she took the difficult and long path. Now she used to go down from a Gujjar dhoka which was at the end of Camp, went down into the rivulet, and crossed to the other side. From this way the Gujjar milkmen and vegetable sellers used to come so a thin track had been created. For a short while, she had to walk on the same track and then walk up the rough slope on the other side before she could reach her Bhagwaan. She held her life in her hands while she was in the rivulet. If perchance her foot did not land smoothly on a boulder, a shriek emerged from her mouth. She used to scold herself. 'Poor one, if your foot had not fallen properly, your limbs and shoulders would have broken. Who would have heard you here? Do you ever tell anyone when you leave home and when you reach here?' While crossing the rivulet she did not turn her eyes anywhere even for a second, leave alone turning them towards right or left. If she had done that, she would have felt dizzy and fallen flat, so she kept looking up into the far-off space with only yellow and muddied boulders. She did not even think about the roaring river during *vaehraath* when water used to rise high.

She was only consoled by the feeling that it would not be long before Bhagwaan Div Shoar was installed. Div Shoar of Div Gaam. There were enough signs of the same happening soon. *Vaehraath* entered but there was no sign of clouds in the sky. Not just the old men and women, everywhere the general public, young and the old were baking in the heat. And Gauri Shauri was busy day and night. Before dawn, she would leave home holding a piece of bread she had tied in cloth overnight, in her armpit. She would finish a lot of the work of the masons and labourers, before the latter had arrived, with the help of the watchman taking out the cement bag from the makeshift shed, watering the bricks, lighting the stove to put water on. Tempted by a cup of tea, the labourers also used to arrive early. Then the prodding of Mataji the whole day did not irritate them.

First of all, Pushkar Nath got the big road up to the temple levelled, so that the truck could move on easily. He used to get the material and hand it over to his mother. She did the work with verve and proper finish as if this aged woman was an expert in construction work. This used to surprise the labourers and the masons as well. Within a few days, they first raised a concrete base on the rivulet side then constructed a wall on that side. Gauri Shauri used to pray to God that until the earth was laid nothing should fall so that she could plant flowers all around. The rain of *vaehraath* would serve as an elixir for the plants. Except for the temple she had no time for thinking about anything nor was her spirit anywhere else. But the indifference of the other people in the camp used to pierce Pushkar's heart. Although from Sheela's conversations Pushkar could sense that everyone was eager about the temple. But what difference could it have made if they had asked him or his mother about the temple?!

Pushkar Nath was very close to Mahraj Krishan and Nanaji. These days even if they met him, nothing beyond customary conversation passed between them. Pushkar Nath became angry and wished he could turn around and call them a couple of names and inform them that he knew what was aching them. 'Even if you don't talk, remember, your interior will burst.' But he was just feeling it from within. Was not telling them anything. He had heard that people were saying that they had got a lot of money through ill means and now, to cast away the evil eye, they had turned some of that money towards the construction of the temple. Pushkar Nath did not heed any of this and remained as he was. He saw them with a scowl on their faces, but he smiled in return. He also saw that the ways of his wife were similar. His mother never complained to him.

But he saw that his wife, despite seeing her mother-in-law working like a labourer and growing weak with each day, did not ask her about well-being. She did not ask Pushkar's mother whether she was tired, or wanted to rest for a day. Never. Nothing.

Sheela used to be alone all day in the room and if anyone asked her, 'How is your mother-in-law?' she knew that the person asking her knew everything and even then she was asking. She would give a diplomatic answer and silence them.

'Is there any lack of ashrams.... All old men and women should do the same as my mother-in-law is doing.'

During the first two to three days of work on the temple Sheela went there with food for her mother-in-law in order to show to her husband. Then she noticed that it was a long assignment and told her husband curtly, 'She is possessed by some genie or under some deep madness.' She stopped going there. Since then Gauri Shauri would pick four to five loaves of bread and some vegetables and leave before her son and daughter-in-law woke up from sleep.

Pushkar Nath smelled that a day would definitely come when the indifference and coldness would go away. 'They will get what we are doing. The affection borne of deep and thick relations cannot dry up in this manner.'

He had also begun to suspect for some days that the work of his mother with fervour and swiftness, which had crossed all limits, might disturb the tranquil atmosphere of the camp. The swiftness gradually expanded, like a ripening boil, and then one day raised its head.

3

After returning tired and exhausted from the temple site, and after having food, when Gauri Shauri sat down, she used to feel lethargic. But sleep did not come to her as it used to in Kashmir after finishing her work at home, returning from the vegetable garden and the fields, or sometimes after the Shankar Mountain *yatra*. That sleep was from the feeling of having achieved something. 'Here in Jammu, in exile, no matter how much work you do, it does not seem much; that is why sleep is also missing.'

She did not understand how her own daughter-in-law spoke the language of the others. 'She believes in what they tell her.' Gauri used to remonstrate to

Bhagwaan, 'Why is her behaviour towards me like this? Don't you remember the behaviour I had towards my own mother- and father-in-law? After all, what can I get from making the temple? I have to fulfil this responsibility. If the strangers don't feel good about me or feel jealous of me, I don't care; my wages are with the Bhagwaan. But she is like my child. If she could just talk to me in a good manner, the women of the camp would not get the opportunity to gossip about our home.'

Gauri Shauri began to contemplate. She recollected that the truth is that what her parents as well as her mother- and father-in-law had told her. They had told her that one should do that through which 'this life and life in the hereafter are successful'. That she considered was the measuring unit with which to weigh people. Even when she had no idea about either close and distant people or birth and faith, she reposed faith in the good and beautiful which the elders did. Whenever she used to hear anything bad about the other houses of Div Gaam, she would change the topic or did not pay attention to what was being said. Was it because of this social behaviour that she was respected by all, consulted by people and involved in all everything good and bad or was it due to something else? She did not know. Actually, she did not even want to know the reason.

Life in the camp of Jammu was not like that of Div Gaam. But whatever Gauri Shauri felt was right and proper, she immediately made her mind to do it. She took time out of the struggle of her life and took upon herself the burden of constructing the temple. She did not feel like asking Sheela to give her a hand for this burden but sometimes she used to feel worried that she was distracting her from work. She shook herself from sinking into deep thought. 'I should not spoil my mind so much that my limbs stop functioning. I should not recollect my childhood and the days of my being a daughter-in-law in the village in Kashmir.'

But the very root idea of building a temple was awakening her connections with her childhood and being a daughter-in-law. Initially, her mother- and father-in-law prevented her from getting involved in the service of the *yatris*[6] of the Shankar Mountain. Later they did not object. Her husband Janki Nath also did not see any danger in that.

---

[6] Pilgrims.

Initially, the Yatra was for a short time. Around forty or fifty people came from the city or the villages on the fourteenth day of *Shraavan*.[7] Ten or twelve houses of Div Gaam usually lent help to them, prepared meals for them, made arrangements for their comfort in their homes so that on the morning of the day of *Punim*[8] they would reach the Siri Cave of Shankar Mountain after a difficult climb of four to five hours. On their way down they would take a bath in the boulder-filled river bed and then reach back by evening. They used to eat *Punim* fast meals in Div Gaam and then boarding the buses reached their homes. Gauri Shauri did not understand when she had become the leader for collecting money for the yatra, or of those women who got various materials and preserved them for the *yatris*. To mend and prepare the track of the *yatris* and get the labourers were assigned to men. Those days Gauri was on cloud nine and used all her energy. Janki Nath used to go along with the *yatris*. But she never mustered the courage to ask him to take her along.

Due to the *yatris* there used to be a lot of hustle and bustle in the village once a year and for domestic women this used to be a fair-like season. Whoever possessed swiftness and ardour, was successful in taking the warmth of the season into the folds of their cold life. Gauri and the other women of her age began to move about their homes and went to the stream which was flowing by the side of the village. Using one or the other excuse they would go to the forest or chat sitting under the chinars on the sloping hilltop.

It seemed Gauri Shauri had some connection with the stream from her previous birth. When she reached close to the stream, she felt herself opening up, all of herself. The stream of Div Gaam was not big but it had spread out on the flat ground in the village. As if she had been hit against rough and tumble before reaching the village, and now after reaching here was spreading her limbs and was going down after taking rest. It seemed as if the limpid and sweet water of the stream was meandering over the milky, green and blue round stones spread out afar, and running away stealthily playing with joyous whistles. The stream was neither too deep nor too shallow anywhere. It was moving over little depths and shallow spots, rollicking and gambolling with the little branches and inviting the

---

[7] Name of a month.
[8] Full moon.

young and the old to a kind of a party. Gauri Shauri raised the *pheran* by holding its edge with both hands tiptoed over the round stones and made a round trip of a fifty to sixty feet wide stream in seconds. Sometimes she put her feet in the water and picked up a pretty round stone in her hand and gazed at it. On this, her friends made fun of her. But she continued with what she wanted to do. She had slyly assembled many round multicoloured stones and hidden them in her home. And then Arundhati would come to her mind.

'Today you will get us beaten. It was fine with you but what have I done to you?' Arundhati was the daughter-in-law of one of the families of Janki Nath's uncles. She had also come to Div Gaam in the same year as Gauri. Gauri responded to her, 'When they beat you, call me.'

'Oh, I will call you! You are yourself under threat there and asking me to call you!' Arundhati replied.

'No, we don't have to die so early. There is yet time for that. Your groom keeps himself in our home for a long time at night talking about things. His parents never tell him anything.' Gauri told her.

'They are men. Get up now. I don't have time for discussions with you.'

Gauri used to leave her chirping friends right away and ran either to her vegetable garden or took away the rice plate from the hands of her mother-in-law and quietly began to sift the chaff. All the anger of her mother-in-law disappeared very quickly.

Gauri gave birth to two daughters before Pushkar Nath but none of them survived. Her uncles would say that she is childish by mind and frosty by the body, her children won't survive. There came a new life in the house with the birth of Pushkar. But it made no difference to Gauri. The elders in the house would rollick and play with the children. Pushkar grew old, went to school, got a job, and was married. Time flew very fast. Gauri used to look behind in time and turned towards the sky with contentment and thanked her Bhagwaan.

The people of Div Gaam were not used to openly expressing it but they did internally feel that over the past eight or ten years their village gained so much importance that the member of the Assembly and the Minister waited for their call to invite him to say goodbye to the *yatris*; the biggest reason for this was Gauri Shauri who had become Lakshmi and Durga. The number of *yatris* had increased to five to six thousand and the name of the village had now been registered with the tourism department. The sense of the beauty of this village located at the foot of the Shankar Mountain had now arisen among the villagers as well. The Shravan Purnima[9] *yatra* was now being called Amarnath Yatra and the boulder-filled river bed on the way down from Sri Cave was now being regarded as nothing short of Gangotri. Now the duty of service to the *yatra* was not restricted to a few homes in the village but the fervour of the people had converted it into a big day for many types of people. No one understood how Aemir Bhat, the Sarpanch of the village, took charge of the arrangements of the *Yatra*. The patwari Sarwanand, who had only been watching the *yatra* from a distance, now asked Janki Nath, 'Which assembly member should I bring?' Ghulam Rasool, who was a secretary in some department in the government secretariat and who had almost forgotten about the village, now he used to arrive in Div Gaam with a team of media men.

Gradually, so much change came in the village that the villagers did not feel the same way. Neither was Gauri Shauri feeling how much she had got involved in things and how important it was. She was content that her mother- and father-in-law, neighbours, and relatives were encouraging her. When she sent Pushkar to school there was no restriction on her going to the stream, sitting under the chinars or going to the forest.

One year the villagers decided to construct a temple. The faith of the *yatris* had deepened. The donation was collected in no time. Four to five homes gave two *marlas*[10] each from their land on the bank of the stream. The people worked collectively and in about two-and-a-half months a concrete room was erected. A few stumps were dug on the side of the stream and a balcony was put up, and on the roof a round top was raised. In the middle of the concrete floor they made a small outlet to take out the water. Gauri lost her sleep and comfort. She sweated due to hard work and felt the shade of contentment.

All this happened very fast as if the village knew that the time was precious because the *Flood*[11] was about to come. The basic structure of the temple was erected but the *Flood* did not give time to install the statue nor did it provide time to perform the ceremony for the installation. The flood

---

[9] The full moon day in the month of Shravan.

[10] A unit of area, equal to 25,2929 square meters.

[11] The *Flood* here is metaphorically used for the sudden peculiarity of circumstances that forced Hindus to migrate.

came with such a fury that Div Gaam and the villages on the other side of the streams and cities were stunned with the devastation. The streams of the forests dried up and the forests disappeared into roads and because of the fear of the *Flood* smiles were lost from faces and eyes turned dry. Those who were from the majority opinion told Janki Nath quietly that it was very difficult for him to survive this 'foreign' *Flood* and they should leave the place for some time.

Late in the evening, Janki Nath went to Kashi Nath.

'Did you hear? We have to leave this place.'

'I know that, but who told you?'

'Don't feel surprised but that will not make any difference. Just tell me whether you are ready.'

No. I told them that I am not ready. And I asked them, 'Why should I leave? Am I so cut off from you?'

'You are separated.... Are you not?'

'Janki Nath.... That is right but this is our birthplace. This blighted place will cut a net for all to be trapped inside. Those who flee and those who ask others to flee.... But everything is false. But we are compelled to cut off all relationships. What shall we do? Even after knowing about everything one does not feel like cutting off this net.'

Kashi Nath knew that all their talk was meaningless. Janki Nath paused for a while as if trying to figure out the meaning of what he said. Then he told him, 'Earth, streams, forests, and mountains.... What will the net of these do? We should have this conversation later on in a leisurely manner? First of all, we should protect ourselves and guard our honour.' These words rose out of his throat with great agony. But he sensed that he was still talking in a convoluted manner. He made himself understand that he could not talk to Kashi Nath in the same direct way as he talked to his wife.

During those days it seemed that before sunset a pall of gloom descended on the whole village. It seemed some evil force came down from the sky in the evening and sealed the mouths and cut the legs.

At night on the day of the departure when no one dared to come out of the house, Gauri went secretly like a thief towards the temple and dropped the colourful collection of her life into the hollow of the temple's outlet: milky pestle, round black stone, coloured *thokuir*, thread tied round blue stones (which she called Shankar). She gazed at them. She whispered as if she was telling them.

'You are the mountains of Div Gaam and you are the paddy fields, plants, and other life forms. When no one cared about us, you used to know our condition. Today the name of the village has been glorified and you are the witness. Now I am handing over the village to you ... All of it ... All of it.'

In the half-darkness Gauri was like a guardian but like an unsuccessful *yeitch*[12] in one corner as if mourning.

She got up and turned. Then an after-thought crossed her mind. She came back and from the same pile of stones picked a blue cylindrical stone. She held it under her *pheran* and left. After leaving the temple, walking over the little raised paths of fields. She felt it had got very late. She felt wavering shadows around her showing her with both hands to leave quickly. Now she was scared and wondered what had happened to her. She recalled having thought about bringing Arundhati with her, but then what had happened, why did she not call her? She clenched her hands tight, and ran and stumbled to her home.

Early morning, before departure, Gauri went to ask permission of Arundhati. She believed that Kashi Nath would not go anywhere. That is what she gathered from the conversations with Arundhati. But there she found the house locked and the door of the stable open.

4

Janki Nath came to Jammu along with his parents and children. For a month, while frenetically looking for a shelter in the refugee camp, they found almost all the people of Div Gaam had assembled in one place. These villagers showed them the way and they were able to get a tent to live in. Janki Nath was at the forefront of making arrangements in the camp. Janki told him cryptically.

'It is fine that even among the fleers you were the first.'

The camp people giggled and said, 'Sadly, that was a foreign flood. At the time of fleeing, who had faith in whom?'

---

[12] An imaginary animal.

Their laughter was a manifestation of their loss of belief. The foreign flood of Kashmir had changed and shaken them all. The 'native storm' of Jammu had cast them out. The first sweltering heat in Jammu took away Gauri's father-in-law and the second her mother-in-law. Early in the new year some insect bit Janki Nath in his bed and nothing could cure him of the poison. The same happened with several others. That broke Gauri's back. Now her only source of light was her Pushkar Nath. She felt that he was her everything. With all her heart she brought up Pushkar Nath's son, Bitto, who was then only twelve years old. Now she felt that this world had changed so much in the last fifteen years than it could in fifty years. Sometimes when her heart broke, with no strength or desire left to live, she prayed to Bhagwaaan to call her called her back to His world.

One day she opened her dusty and rusted trunk. From Kashmir, she had only brought this trunk and since then used to keep it close to her. There she found two things. One, the post-office passbook of her husband and second, that blue cylindrical stone which she had picked from the *pranalyi*[13] of the temple.

Janki Nath had fallen sick for only two days. Before his death he called Pushkar Nath to him. He told him that his disabled self would remain doing the rounds of Div Gaam in Kashmir but enjoined him to fulfil his mother's desire of building the temple. With eyes filled with tears, Pushkar Nath put his hands upon his father's hands, and then his father passed away.

Sheela initially was glad that her mother-in-law was gradually forgetting her husband. The passbook and temple would also be forgotten soon. But she did not know that her husband would be Gauri's well-wisher. Pushkar Nath kept the spirit of the temple alive in his mother and the latter felt encouraged. She kept Div Gaam alive even in Jammu. The village had shrunk in her *Thokuir* and the *Thokuir* had become Div Shuir. When the camp people heard about Div Shuir from the mouth of Sheela, they asked her in wonder:

'Where is Div Shuir here? We have not heard of any deity of this name here?'

'People remembered that they had not yet started the installation of the deity in the village and they had to flee.'

---

[13] Outlet of the holy water.

People in the refugee camp enjoyed chatting about Gauri. They would say, 'It is said that Gauri Shauri rested the statue in the same night in the temple . . . when we were preparing to flee early in the morning.'

But some were smarter. They used to say, 'This is now meaningless talk. She has to make a temple here, let her make it. Let her call it Div Shuir or Shiv Shuir. It will not make any difference.'

The camp people never believed that Gauri single-handedly installed the statue in the temple there and then brought it here to Jammu. They felt as if Gauri Shauri had started a fable by the name of Div Shuir.

Sheela listened to all and wondered on what pretext her mother-in-law would build the temple. But Gauri Shauri did not pay any heed to people. She used to say that one day Div Shuir would get around their throats and nice things would come out of their mouths.

How far had Gauri Shauri's story extended surprised even her, and the people were caught unawares.

5

On that day there was a lot of hue and cry. A crowd gathered outside the room of Kashi Nath. Worry had elongated the faces of all.

Arundhati was restless. She had not slept for eleven days. She had a high fever which was not subsiding. Now she was mumbling something inane, getting up time and again, dizzying and falling down again. She was repeating only one thing. 'Div Shuir! Div Shuir! Here it comes, Div Shuir! Div Shuir! Div Shuir!!'[14]

Hearing this name, the relatives of Arundhati would laugh, and listening to what they used to call Gauri Shauri's 'story' from the tongue of sick Arundhati, scared them. 'First Gauri got possessed by this, and showed Arundhati the way to the temple, and has struck down Arundhati, and no one knows what is going to happen next.'

Doctors used to say that something has captured her inner self. Their experience told them that those people who were used to reflecting on nuances of life are worried by even small changes in the nature of social relations. This was not understood by Kashi Nath or anyone else although

---

[14] A reference to the deity.

they understood that Arundhati was remembering her village in Kashmir and the loss of the village temple had made her homesick. But what could they do?!! They were saying that she should be admitted to a mental hospital, but how would that makeup for the loss. 'She is under some magic charm. Take her to Kashmir.... Take her to her village.' Everyone was giving this counsel.

Gauri Shauri also came to know. She said that once her fever came down, she will stop saying inane things. But when she heard that Arundhati was talking about Div Shauri, she became alert. Pushkar Nath had brought in a vehicle-load of earth. He did not see his mother waiting outside as used to be the case but she was lying on the bedstead in the shed. He panicked.

Gauri stretched her hands towards the setting sun, and words came out of her, 'Oh my Bhagwaan! Arundhati has got the responsibility of many members, simple and honest. Keep her under your protection.' Then she turned to her son, 'I think they will complete the wall by day after tomorrow.'

This was known to Pushkar Nath as well.

'Yes, I know. So?'

'Tomorrow you do not have to go anywhere. Get up from sleep a little earlier. They might need iron and cement. First I will go to Arundhati's home and then come here.'

Pushkar Nath felt that his mother was not talking now in the same manner as she used to in the past, in an open and glad manner. She says a word for the outside world and holds two within and keeps reflecting on the latter. He was also feeling tired. The work had stretched out more than they had expected. On the one hand, was the strain of work and on the other the whispers of the people of the camp. 'Arundhati is ill, and now what has my mother to do by going there. Up till now, she was working away from the sight of all so that she did not have to encounter anyone of them. Now, why is she going to enliven their gossip and backbites by visiting them? There the conversation will not remain only about Arundhati. And when her conversation begins with mother then there is no end.'

The sun set. The labourers began to collect their tools for the day. As usual, Gauri Shauri gave instructions to the watchman about the work after evening and what he had to do tomorrow. 'You should take the cement inside the shed, scratch the bucket clean of the material used in it.

Tomorrow morning, the truck will reach here, fill the drum for them, silt has accumulated inside the tank, clean it up.' Pushkar Nath was seeing all this and thinking, 'Mother, you should have been a man. What is a chief engineer compared to you?! Nothing.'

Gauri Shauri left after folding her hands in front of the blue *Thokuir* which was placed on a wooden stand inside the shed.

Pushkar Nath was waiting for her outside. The labourers had left a long time before. Just then, a conversation at a distance could be heard. After the sunset, not even jackals used to howl in this wilderness, let alone human beings. It was strange.

Pushkar Nath tried to hear the sounds. It was clear that some people were walking towards him. He turned towards his mother. She was also alerted to this sight. Both of them came out a little. They noticed that a few inmates of the camp were coming towards them. When they came close Pushkar Nath recognized them all and said aloud as if to himself, 'Maharaj Krishan, Gopi Nath. Kishan Ji. Nanna Ji and following them is Jawa Laal.... What has happened to them today? Why have they come here?'

'Don't worry. It will be all good,' his mother told him without fully opening her mouth. All of them came and stood before Gauri Shauri. They complained. 'Mother, what sins have we committed? You have abandoned us. You are never at home nor do you know what is happening in the camp. After all, are we not your own people? Don't we have hope in you?'

Pushkar Nath felt that they are making a scene out there, but Gauri Shauri was wondering that so many days had passed with her regularly coming here before daybreak and returning home in darkness, till now everything was as usual in the colony, what worry had befallen them that brought them here.

'Not at all my children. We have hope. You are my children. Are you not my progeny? What happened? Is everything fine?'

Jawa Lal was standing at the back. He seemed very disheartened. Gauri asked him, 'Jawa Lal! How is your Arundhati?'

As if Jawa Lal was waiting for the same cue, he wept loudly and then fell at the feet of Gauri Shauri.

'Mother, you are the *Bhagwati*.[15] We are all mean and of low caste.... But you should forgive us. Please get us out of this.'

---

[15] Goddess.

All of this was unfolding like in a drama, and Gauri Shauri remained stupefied. She looked towards Pushkar Nath. Pushkar Nath picked up Jawa Lal and held him tight against himself, 'What happened Jawa Lal?!! As if you have lost heart. Does no one fall ill?'

Maharaj Krishan explained, 'He is deeply worried about his mother.'

Gauri said, 'I know that. I was telling Pushkar a while ago that I would go tomorrow to see Arundhati.'

Jawa Lal folded his hands before her. 'No mother. You will have to come now. Along with us.'

Nanna Ji said, 'For the last two days her condition has worsened. We can't say how she will be tomorrow.'

Arundhati was Gauri Shauri's childhood friend. She had not forgotten that they had come to Div Gaam as daughters-in-law almost at the same time. She became worried after hearing this. She regretted that she got herself so entangled in this net of the temple to have forgotten about her surroundings. 'My kith and kin, with which is made my world, have got cut off from me.'

Jawa Lal saw that Gauri Shauri's face bore signs of some hope. He said, 'Mother, Arundhati is only looking for you.'

'May my life be laid for her! My God will protect her. Wait I will take for her the elixir of my God's feet.' She went inside the shed and in a vessel got a spoonful or two of the water.

'God, you guard her, you guard her. Arundhati used to pray to you in the village, here also she has been your ardent worshipper ... You should protect her.'

It seemed as if Gauri was running. Her exhaustion did not stop her feet.

Maharaj Krishan and Gopi Nath were walking behind others. They were telling Pushkar Nath, "'These women are not straight.... Since you have started work, they were telling all kinds of things against her. They were taunting her. 'If Gauri Shauri is your friend why are you not asking her?' All the conferences were taking place in Arundhati's room.

On top of that do you know how simple and pure Arundhati is? She had planned many times that she would go to the temple during the daytime and see for herself.... These women did not allow her to do that.'"

Pushkar Nath was slowly untangling their words. But he did not reply to any of it. Neither saying yes nor no. He wished to tell them, 'If they are women, what about you people, you were men. Was your behaviour any different from theirs? You are worse than women.' But he thought the occasion was not appropriate.

When Arundhati saw Gauri Shauri, the energy of a genie returned to her body. One who did not have the strength to touch anything suddenly got up and hugged Gauri, when the latter came close to her. A shout came out of her. 'Mother! Mother Bhagwati!' And she started kissing her hands and feet.

Gauri Shauri was all sweat not because of what Arundhati was doing but because of seeing herself becoming the centre of a crowd of people. She asked for water.

Arundhati's daughter-in-law gave her a vessel of water which she gulped down without break. Then she said, 'Why have you converted her to wood?! What if she had a fever? Come bring Mughal tea[16] and Kulchi.'[17]

Arundhati did not move her gaze from Gauri. Gauri gave her tea with a spoon and she had it without any difficulty. Arundhati felt life return to her.

'Kaakin[18] got well! Kaakin got well! Mataji fed her Kulchi with her hand.... Today after eight days she swallowed some food .... Mataji is truly an incarnation of God.' The message went across the whole camp. Whoever came inside the room did not leave. Only hearkening to what would fall from the mouth of Gauri Shauri. What kind of movement Mataji would make. Men were putting their heads through door and windows, watching, and saying, 'For so long has she been close to the Bhagwaan ... going round and round the Div Shuir.'

Now the name of Div Shuir was not the source of fun and sarcasm against Gauri Shauri.

Jawa Lal turned to Gauri Shauri, 'Mataji! What ten doctors could not do for Kaakin, you have done with just one look. Otherwise, she has remained transfixed in just one place for such a long time. Fever had made her restless. If she had not uttered your name repeatedly, we would not have given you the trouble of coming here.'

---

[16] A kind of tea, with a mix of some dry fruits and spices.
[17] A kind of bread used in Kashmir.
[18] Sometimes a reference to the brother's wife.

Mahraj Krishan said, 'You must be tired Mataji. The whole day without rest.... It is because of the strength bestowed on you by Bhagwaan, otherwise it is not possible for anyone.'

It seemed that Arundhati had closed her eyes for a doze and Gauri Shauri began to get up. But Jawa Laal caught her feet, 'No Mataji. Please tell Kaakin that by tomorrow she will be fine and I will take you to temple.'

'What is the big deal about that? Is that why you were doing all of this?'

Up to this point, Krishan Lal was quietly seated. Now he got up and looking mockingly at the women, he said, 'Kaakin opened our eyes. We were torn by jealousy.... Mataji, you should forgive us. We are sinners.' He went towards Gauri Shauri and sat weeping in front of her.

At that time Arundhati shouted, 'May my life be sacrificed on you Div Shauri!!' Then again she lapsed into a semi-conscious state.

Gauri stroked her hair and face, 'How are you feeling Arundhati? I am Gauri.'

Arundhati opened her eyes and gazed at her.

Gauri Shauri thought, 'It is all due to the power of "my" Div Shuir. I was thinking that until I install it in the temple, I would not tell anyone I had got it from Div Gaam but Div Shuir wished otherwise. It did not keep itself hidden. Before me it reached Arundhati. Now why should I not proclaim it myself...?' She said, 'Div Bhagwaan has come to us here. Now we will install him on *Kartik punim*.[19] All evil is gone. You have become all right ... I will take you someday to the temple. It will take some fifteen to twenty-one days to complete. When the wall is erected then it won't take much time.'

Did Arundhati hear all of this? Her eyes had grown heavy.

Salt tea was brought after a while. First for Gauri Shauri and then was given to Pushkar Nath. Then some women had it.

Gauri was suddenly feeling lost due to this kind of welcome but did not give any hint of it to others. She talked to the women in a nice manner as if the whole fault was hers that without telling anyone and without consulting anyone, she went about building the temple. She had also heard that people were saying a number of things about her but folding her hands before the blue Thokar she was praying: 'My dear Bhagwaan! By taking them out of Kashmir how much punishment you have given them.

---

[19] Full moon day of the months of Kartik.

That is enough. After this you should protect them. Don't pay heed to what others are saying.'

Mahraj Krishan took Pushkar out to a side and told him, 'It was Jawa Lal who came almost running to say that Kaakin was mumbling and asking to be taken to Gauri Shauri and to Bhagwaan Div Shuir.' She had a high fever and was not in a condition even to be taken to the hospital. Initially, she was only saying something which we did not pay attention to but later we felt perhaps that was her cure. She said that Gauri Shauri is the Bhagwati. And she went on to worship her. She began to read *Leelas*.[20] She said that Div Bhagwaan had come and was sitting in her home. 'Take me to her home or it will destroy everything of yours.' It went on until today the doctor said that bring Gauri here. 'Now don't you see what magic has been wrought. We do not listen to our own. Today Mataji came for Kaakin like a god-incarnate.'

On the other side, Jawa Lal was telling Gauri Shauri, 'Mataji ... Now it won't take much time to make the temple. We were blind. Kaakin opened our eyes. Now you will not be alone. We are now just like your own Pushkar Nath. We will sacrifice ourselves for you. We will give our life.... You brought our Div Bhagwaan here. That is no joke! Even if you use us as bricks and stone, we will not mind.'

Gauri Shauri felt herself melting. She embraced Jawa Lal.

'May my life be sacrificed for you? You are closer to me than Pushkar Nath. Bhagwaan will protect you under his feet. In the same way as he had put his shade for you.'

Then she stroked Arundhati's head and told her, 'There also you were rubbing your forehead near the feet of Bhagwaan. With what love and affection did you make the temple! You installed the bell and the container! But it was not the wish of Bhagwaan to stay there. Bhawaan was favourable toward our village. When there were killings on all sides, he did not allow anyone to touch even a child. But when the flood reached near our feet, and he appeared in our dream, then we left the village after circumambulation around the temple, and continuously looking back with desirous eyes.'

While saying this Gauri Shauri felt choked with tears.

---

[20] Literally, means a play. An important concept in Hinduism, the whole cosmos being a leela, a dance, or energy, a drama staged by the Absolute.

It was clear that Arundhati had only shared her dream with Gauri Shauri. People were wondering that despite his repeated negative response Kashi Nath had left the village before anyone else. But today things had become clear.

Jawa Lal told Gauri: 'That was the cause of all this behaviour with Kaakin, Mataji. On the day of the departure, she was weeping all day and then kept on weeping even here. She had scary dreams every night. Was saying all kinds of wild things about the temple.'

'Actually, she was homesick. As if she had left her suckling child behind,' one of the women in the group said.

There was silence. They were listening to the snoring of Arundhati. No one could believe that she was asleep.

Gauri Shauri said after some time, 'Dears, this is the wish of Bhagwaan. He only gave me encouragement and strength.' Pushkar Nath said the same thing. 'If Mataji had not remained steadfast, how could I have started it? Sometimes visiting the Tehsildar, sometimes the patwari and sometimes the MLA, all these visits with pleas tired me out. I told myself many times that I should stop this. But what could I have told Mataji. It is all because of her.'

Jawa Lal had gone out. After a while he came back with a big bag and dropped that at the feet of Gauri Shauri.

'Mataji, whatever happened until now should be put behind, we have all sought your forgiveness. Now this is our token contribution of leaves and flowers for the temple. I hope you will not deny this and break our hearts.'

Gauri Shauri took her feet behind and held back her *dhoti* with her hand, 'No, not at all. Don't say that.... When I need anything I will ask you.'

When Jawa Lal, Krishan Ji, and Nannaji and others, along with some women, pleaded with Gauri Shauri, the latter became restless. As if the battle of Mahabharata was being fought in her mind. She felt as if they were trying to put her down under their favour. She felt a little irritated and tried again to get up.

'No. Don't compel me. Allow me to install my Thokuir. After that whatever makes Him happy, do that with Him. Either you can use ours on him or we can use yours.'

It was clear that the people sitting there were upset with the denial of Gauri Shauri. But Pushkar Nath sensed that his mother was feeling restless. If she could not accept the money of her own grandson, how could she accept their money? Until now they might have been saying all kinds of things, and now some kind of faith had emerged out of them.

There was exhaustion and fatigue on Gauri's face which had begun to change into contentment and happiness in the house of her friend. But now with this compensation, she felt shaken. Before leaving she took out a vessel from the bag, in which she had kept the *amrit*.[21] She nudged Arundhati, 'This is the leftover *amrit* from the Div Shuir. I offer Him water in the morning and by evening it has become dry. Today when Jawa Lal told me about your sickness, I saw the wide plate wet. These are those few spoonfuls.'

With a spoon, she put the *amrit* into Arundhati's mouth. Taking the drops down her throat, she held her hand and began to look at her with yearning eyes.

'No, now it is late. Tomorrow I will come again.'

Gopi Nath spoke up. He was the eldest among the camp people.

'You did not listen to us. Now she is telling you. She is your childhood friend. You have together played under the chinars of Div Gaam and on the banks of the river. Because of you two, the foundation stone of the temple had been laid. First, you had made a shed and then a concrete temple ... Here we have been trapped in the nets of life. We have abandoned each other.... Now it appears Bhagwaan has himself come to our aid. Otherwise we had forgotten even him.'

The elder was wisely speaking. All were silently listening and nodding their heads. Gauri was also in deep thought, feeling that they had already decided that she had got some statue of Bhagwaan from Div Gaam to this camp. 'Why don't they use their mind that we had not installed any statue there? Shall I tell them the truth? Though Arundhati is a goddess-figure. Maybe she has dreamed about the same.'

Gopi Nath's white beard was increasing the brightness of his fair face. Keeping his talk going, he said in the end, 'Mataji, you Bhagwati. The leader does not reject the contribution of the disciple.'

---

[21] Elixir or holy water.

Sheela was quiet all this while. Now she was impatient. She signalled to her husband something to the effect that, 'If your mother does not accept it, why don't you receive it?'

It was unclear to Pushkar Nath whether these people were being honest or ostentatious. He thought it was time for him to speak clearly otherwise these very people who were speaking so softly and earnestly, saying a lot of nice things, would tomorrow make up a lot of stories, and say a number of things.

He told Jawa Lal, 'Wait a second. Are you not giving this money for the temple?'

Jawa Lal could not believe. 'Yes. What else do you think? This is our contribution for this good work. Of us all.'

The matter was now clear. This was the money they had collected and when Mataji heard about this. Puskar Nath addressed Gopi Nath in a soft tone, 'Elder one, do you know how much affection and love my father had for Div Gaam? He was not so much worried about the land and property which he had left behind there but he was upset that he had left behind an incomplete temple. Before passing away he told his wife that she should fulfil his desire of constructing the temple for Bhagwaan. At the time of retirement, he had put his G P Fund earnings in the post office and had made his wife the nominee. That amount has doubled by now. My mother has also been saving her pension money. Till we have this money we will carry on the construction. When the temple is built, it will not be just ours ... !'

Hearing this the whole room turned enthusiastic and Gopi Nath told Gauri Shauri, 'Salutations be all to you! Congratulations to you and your son!'

Due to the noise in the room Arundhati again opened her eyes and with some signs called Krishan Lal and gave him a bag. But he told her to keep it with her. 'We will see later.' He turned towards Gauri Shauri, 'Whatever you tell us now, even if you beat us that will be to us like an offering, a blessing. But will you allow us to come there when it is complete ... ?'

Gauri Shauri had tears in her eyes. 'May my life be sacrificed on you! Is Bhagwaan just mine? He will guard us all in this alien land.'

6

Now Gauri Shauri did not need to remain at the workplace from morning till evening, neither did Pushkar Nath only have to do the running around. Now there were more people to look after and arrange the work than were needed. A new life was infused into the camp. Now the blistering sun was not blinding the inmate's eyes nor was the cloud darkening their sight. The severed village of Div Gaam in Kashmir was in their mind and the cool shade of the river-side was in their eyes. After the heat came the monsoon. The rivulet began to roar but the concrete base of the temple remained firm against the waves like the determination of Gauri and brick by brick the construction continued. In addition to Gauri's money, it remained unknown from where the people got money for the construction. The people of the neighbouring village were also inspired, and gradually got busy with the work. From the side of the temple the tap had reached the village, the track had become a road so that the vehicles reached the village and even to the Camp.

The temple was complete and after fixing the day, a Havvan was performed. It became an occasion of a big fair on that day. After the Havvan, the Bhagwaan Div Shuir was put on the pedestal which until then Gauri had protected with her heart. The blue round beautiful stone set tears rolling from the eyes of the onlookers and a chorus began, 'Div Bhawaano!! Oh, our Div Shuir!! Our Div Gaam Village!!!'

After receiving the handful of the Havvan, Gauri closed her eyes and told her late husband through her spirit. 'Hope you are jealous of these other people for taking a part of the water from the installation of the Bhagwaan and depriving your wife of the same. See how many with their raised hands are praying to Bhagwaan to provide cool shade in the other world.'

After reciting the *Shantih* when the handfuls were being delivered to the sacred fire, a jeep pulled over outside. It was Sayein Das who had arrived on the scene. Two people with him brought a sackful of flowers from the jeep and brought it inside.

He went to Pushkar Nath, 'I am late. Still no problem. These few flowers will be of use to the faithful in the coming days.'

He went to pay obeisance to the sacred fire and there his eyes caught sight of Gauri Shauri. Both were looking at each other. As if Sayein Das had seen her somewhere. Then Pushkar Nath addressed him, 'This is my mother ... Actually this is done by.'

Sayein Das broke in, 'Yes, yes, I know. What shall I say; I am ashamed that I could not come even once.'

He went down at her feet. Now she had recognized him and the allegation of stealing flowers had come to her mind. She apprehended he might recall the same. She just told him, 'May you continue to live!!'

He went and returned with a pan full of flowers from a sack. 'Mataji, please offer these flowers to Bhagwaan on my behalf. The sins I had committed on that day will be washed off.'

Gauri Shauri blushed up to her ears. But she held her nerve.

'Sin? Which sin, my son? Pushkar Nath says that you have done so much work for the temple ... The credit of the temple goes to you.'

'Oh no, Mataji. My heart is feeling heavy ever since the day I prevented you from taking the flowers.'

Now Gauri Shauri felt pity for him. She wondered how rich this man is and yet how pure of heart. 'Bhagwaan is not convinced by nothing.' Her heart was also purified and she told him with a smile. 'No, son! What heaviness of heart? See how many flowers, on the interior of the wall.' She pointed towards the flower beds which she had made.

Sayein Das was embarrassed when he saw that. For a while he was struck dumb. Then he said. 'But Mataji! .... But these flowers are not to be plucked but for decoration only. The flowers to be offered to the Bhagwaan will come only from me. It is my responsibility to bring them here.'

Hearing this, everyone present there appreciated and clapped, and Gauri Shauri put her hand on his head. She put the other hand on Jawa Lal's head. She heaved a deep sigh of relief, and addressed herself, as if simultaneously telling the nearby standing Pushkar Nath, 'Nath ji. God knows how many people's wishes have been fulfilled today as soon as the holy fire reached its full form. Today my wish of this lifetime has also been fulfilled. Today from each fiber of my self prayer is coming out. Now I have just one craving, just one craving....

In Div Gaam there was one umbrella-like Chinar providing shade to Div Shuir. Here also we should plant a chinar sapling.'

Gauri did not complete her sentence. Her eyes were searching something beyond the walls of the temple, in the far sky. All of them were silent and probing for something in their private skies.

Sayein Das could not understand what sorrow descended on this happy ambience all of a sudden. He asked Pushkar Nath, and the latter made him understand. After getting the reason a smile crossed his face, and he said, 'Hey Mataji! You have brought the whole holy place here. There must be nothing left now.... Yes, chinar. Please leave that and don't talk about that.'

But holding her hand tight on his head and bowing before her, Jawa Lal, with closed eyes was thinking. As if he was telling her. 'Mataji. What you are for us, this big chinar could not be more than that.'

Afterword

The suffix given to any word in grammar either changes or enhances the meaning of the word. Which means that the root characteristic of a word is that it is possible to enhance its meaning and by adding various diacritical marks, it can give different meanings. I am adding this afterword to my stories so that their meaning can be supplemented. However, these stories are not of someone else, so that I can begin to find flaws in them or shower praise on them. I can state an opinion about them only as their reader, or as their critic.

At the time of publishing these stories I had asked myself 'Why did you write these stories?' The conditions represented in these stories are unique, their characters are unique, and the usage of language is also unique, but why is that so? 'By writing about them are you trying to throw light on some special national aspect or is there some other reason?' I raised the questions; hence I had to provide answers to them. I cannot escape answering them. It is said in Kashmir that when the carpenter is forced to show his performance, he takes recourse to all kinds of tricks.

I have written most of these short stories during the last fifteen years. It means that home is remembered when out of home, pining for Kashmir when out of Kashmir, going in dreams to places where in reality we could not have gone, creating such characters which might not have been otherwise possible. But when I look back, I see that I have also incorporated those stories which were written before the last fifteen years but which were fit for this collection because in them is the same concern, reflecting the same pain of restlessness. For example the story 'Curfew' (it is actually part of the collection 'Aeichar Waalan peth Koah'),[1] 'Hum Safar' (part of the collection 'treikuinjal'; there are some signs of the anguish of home in this story),[2] 'Raev maeit Myaanei',[3] another 'Reish Naam' and

---

[1] 'Aeichar Waalan peth Koah' means 'Mountain on the Eyelashes'.
[2] *Treikuinjal* means Triangular.
[3] It means Lost Meanings.

'Choaekdhar' (they are part of the collection 'Raev maeit Myaanei').[4]
The stories 'Snow' and 'Layered Earth' were written a long time ago, but
I have put them in this collection due to the similarity of theme. It implies
that in this collection there is uniqueness due to the matching themes of
the stories. 'Layered Earth', 'Panjtantra', and 'Measureless' have the same
theme; however, compared to the theme, the idioms and sayings call for
deeper attention in them.

> I cannot say that any one of the short stories in this collection is trying
> to convey any unintended point in any non-traditional phrase-
> ology. Although it is a reality that all these stories are trying to con-
> jure numerous images and dimensions of an aspect of life, an aspect
> which is conspicuous by the absence of home for a community.
> All the entrapping situations encircle the characters suddenly and
> against their expectations.
>
> The alien space and atmosphere away from home of most of the char-
> acters have been shaped during the last ten to fifteen years. All the
> people present on this foreign land feel that their world shrunk but
> its vast scope is present in their minds. Anyway, this is just one as-
> pect of that life which is trying hard to maintain its sense of balance
> and consciousness after getting disconnected from the original
> land under its feet in Kashmir. These people who live this uncer-
> tain life are feeling the pain of that life as well which is there across
> the mountains in Kashmir, encircled by restlessness and apprehen-
> sions; a life that has lost a sense of direction and is not able to say
> anything in a decisive manner.
>
> My sympathetic reader can find a peculiar aspect of these characters
> has been evoked, which he had not even perhaps speculated about.
> Especially that aspect, which arises in rituals and customs after a
> human being is suddenly removed from one cultural context and
> deposited into another. Whether it is the refugee camp, the bad
> weather condition, or the wait for the fruit of a tree which has been
> uprooted and planted in an alien soil, or the fear for life during day
> and night after the knock on the door, etc., all of these only provide

---

[4] Some of the stories mentioned in the Afterword are not in the book. So, it seems some of
them have been dropped from this collection. Perhaps forgot to edit the afterword.

the raw material for the creation of a condition in the short story. You will see how the victims of these conditions react to such situations. Often these responses become vulnerable to stylisations. Both writing and psychological stylisation.

In the short story titled 'Separation', Roshan Lal is stunned after the death of his mother in the refugee camp at Jammu. He talks in a broken manner about a time in the past which does not seem to have any connection with his present situation. Finally, to take him away from such unnatural mental condition a man summons courage and tells him in a loud voice. 'Roshan Lal, where is that *Kaakh*?[5] What are you talking about? Kaakh has passed away twenty years ago. Today your mother has passed away. Your mother, Arni. Your father had only seen the cool, shady village (in Kashmir). Your mother saw both the cool of the village as well as the fiery wasteland here in Jammu. Today you are free of both. Your separation is complete.'

It is not necessary to strengthen the point that the break which took place in the 1990s between the past and the present was altogether different from all types of such breaks in the past. It is no surprise therefore that in the foreign soil of Jammu, Roshan Lal is caught in the dilemma of being like a door which, thanks for having come off a bit, is on the one hand dragging on and on the other still stuck in the threshold. He has realized that he is completely separated from his real self. This tragedy can shake his mental balance. On the other hand, deep in his consciousness which is thousands of years old, a worm is still alive and is giving him the assurance, 'One day I will become a big fish and pull your boat so that you can cross the ocean.' Before he is able to cross the ocean, Roshan Lal is keeping alive the hope of a condition of life with other characters (Muslims), on the other bank of the ocean. Most of the short stories in this collection have taken birth in similar moments as that of the mental make-up of Roshan Lal.

• Some people called the disturbed state of the last fifteen years as the clash of civilizations, and compared it with a similar condition of some place, of some other time. However, I do not agree

---

[5] Father or sometimes an elder brother.

with this point of view. According to me civilization is not so much dependent on religion as it is on language and race. Now so far as languages are concerned, how are Rasheed and Roshan different from each other? But, yes, so long as they preserve their language. I go through a lot of spiritual anguish that the native language is not given due regard on either side of Jammu and Kashmir. It is not given due value in Kashmir nor is it trusted in Jammu. When value and trust go away from a language, then if religion is alive and ticking, civilisation will not remain with the people. Anyway.

The same civilization rooted in language provides a bridge to my characters and lets them cross from one side to the other and gives birth to such situations which take place and will continue to occur in the future. I am not a social scientist or any *Jyotish*[6] of the political future that I can provide any way to weld the multi-dimensional separation that has occurred. Perhaps there might be a way or probably not. Anyway, characters in my stories, who have borne the struggle and restlessness of the last fifteen years, are true, because their miseries, pain, compulsions, and mental apprehensions are based on truth. The attempt of my stories is that they evoke this truth of pain and suffering purely on the humanitarian plane so that the reader does not only remain a spectator but also carries a little of their pain.

After having written the stories when I felt that the title of some of them are that of the fundamental elements of nature: Earth, Fire, Air, Water. I tried to search my mind but found that the conceptual moments have moved far away. However, the conceptual imagination does go far away but logic aids us in studying ourselves. I feel that the cure for our ailments is also from these basic natural elements because my characters eat the same food on this side of the bank, and are warmed and cooled by the same climatic changes, and are breathing the same air as they breathed on the other side. Even after all this I do not try to propose to put forward any solution. I just raise questions and try to explain the attitudes of characters to those questions. I do not wish that my reader rests without giving any thought to the situations. I wish that he continuously remains

---

[6] Astrological fortune teller.

awake. I do not claim to be known as the historian of any nationality, but I will definitely write about the contemporary nation because that gives me the tongue to write my stories.

The character of my stories is that home-separated Kashmiri whom I have seen and understood during the last fifteen years. He is starkly living in the so-called migrant camps of the city of Jammu or in the narrow cramped rented rooms. This collection is a best-effort-possible representation of the life of the homeless Kashmiri. His thoughts, the fear, and hope present in his heart, his dreams and reality are to a great extent representative of the dreams and realities of the Kashmiris present here in Jammu. However, his condition can be only understood in the context of the hope and fear which are faced by the whole Kashmiri nation, irrespective of faith. That is why you will notice that the situation of all stories is, one way or the other, evoking a part or portion of the total life of Kashmir. To understand a part or portion it is important to refer to the general or to understand the general (situation).

Although in some stories, the narrator is the character himself, that is, he presents the point of view but the story 'Dakhl' is a little different. So it is important to talk separately about this short story. The focus of this story is 'we' which is the plural of 'I'. 'We' are now the residents or refugees of an alien land (or exiled who are now nicknamed 'migrants'). They give arguments in their defence during the course of the stories because there is an allegation against them that they are interfering in the private life of one Usha, and are coming in the way of her reunion with her husband, Autar. When the story begins Autar Krishan has come to his wife after seven years, not actually for his wife but at the death of his mother-in-law. 'We' (that is, the camp dwellers) are both surprised and angry that he left his wife here in a refugee camp and himself stayed back in Kashmir, with God knows whom, and in which manner. Even after reaching the Camp, Autar does not seem to comprehend the situation. Finally, the situation takes a turn and this truth is revealed that the social, or you can call them the close relations of the garden of saints (Kashmir) do shine forth which have disappeared under the dust of the incompatible conditions of the time. But the problem would not have been resolved in this manner if it had not been incited by us (some distant near ones). That is the intervention of the point of view of the story proved right.

There are many narrators of the story but in this story their voices are presented through one representative voice, and offer only one story. But being a collective voice, we cannot prove their individual character. In the same way whatever is said about the central characters like Usha and Autar by their 'close but alien-to-each-other' figures, even that cannot gain much depth. Their characteristics can only be stated by their outward behaviour. By keeping in mind these issues, we can properly explain and understand this story. This comes to me also as a student of my own story.

Through the theme of the story or due to the central idea we see that what happens in the story, or what the writer is trying to convey is that the interference of the 'close but alien-looking' person can also sometimes strengthen the social ties. That can also bring a family closer and forge afresh the links of relationships. A little bit of interference is important otherwise the families will soon disunite and scatter before time. The stress of the modern life does give us material for such changes. Even we cannot save ourselves from this reality. By entering into our entire existence and moving through our all parts, these devastating changes will not leave anything undone. Although we have several other kinds of pain, disturbance, and fire to endure, Kashmir has been crushed by these agonies and burnt by fire. No cool shade, which could have given us space to rest during the journey, can survive under these situations. We have been encircled and imprisoned by the stresses and the self-made pains of the so-called modern life. From this situation a similar kind of 'Intervention' which is collective in nature and has a connection with our traditional thought pattern, can rescue us. I do not have any intention to talk about any philosophy in the story nor do I have any need of that kind. These issues came up when Hindi translation of the story was read in a meeting of Sahitya Akademi; some of my friends turned the discussion in this direction and also encouraged me. Otherwise my short story will narrate her story. You just read.

The last long short story 'Yeeri luukh pari luukh' (Gauri's Div Gaam) gives an indication of the unique cultural behaviour of Kashmiri Hindus living in Jammu. And that refers to the strategies which any nation makes in order to keep alive the community outside the native land. In addition to giving Kashmiri names to mohallas and habitations, almost all the ashrams of the *sants* of Kashmir have been reconstructed in Jammu.

I do not know whether artificial structures of Tul Mul and even that of Parbath Teeraths have been established in Jammu due to disillusionment of not being able to return home or an effort to build traditional pillars of belief against prevailing disappointment. It is obvious that these holy places were providing some purpose to the life of the believers while living in Kashmir. The significance of these ashrams, dharamshalas re-emerged with the shaking of the foundations of life. What may be the individual psychology and collective approach behind the recreation of these holy places in Jammu? To understand that led to the creation of this short story. Earlier also I have written some short stories which grew long during the course of writing. However, this story has been consciously made long; there is a spreading out and breadth in this story but in terms of its theme and approach it is a short story and not a novelette.

A short story is a narrative genre and hence it is closely connected to the references of time and place. In addition to that, it bears the culture of its time along with its speed. From this point of view both the novel and the short story have a dense association with birth, death, and the events of life as compared to that of poetry. Perhaps it has to bear a greater responsibility because a narrative (even if it is a collection) shows people and reminds them that their present continues to flow from their past. The narrative lends a special feature to our culture exactly in the same way as culture shapes our narratives. Previously it used to be in the long legends and epics (for example, *Ramayan, Mahabharat, Shahnama, Odyssey*) in a stark and in a mixed and jumbled fashion. In the modern period this was carried forward by the short story and the novel. A delicacy and an abstractness came in the modern narrative due to which the continuity broke or was broken in order to create some special effect. However, overall, in both novel and short story (fiction) the element of narration remained present. The cause of the movement was the collectivity of people or a particular attitude of nations or the evocation of any direction, or evoking its painful picture. As a story writer, in front of me is spread out the vast canvas of the known surroundings of my society. If I am referring to some unfamiliar things but the basic reference remains that of the known canvas.

Generally, nationalities select their national poets. A belief which is actually a kind of a supposition is gradually evoked and the people discover their national expression in that poet. This happens among the ordinary people who do not have any understanding of poetry. When people feel that they are in some collective danger and take part in protests and demonstrations, ready to sacrifice themselves, without knowing about the intentions of the organizers, the poetry of these poets ignites their sense of pride and sometimes even compels them to put their lives at stake. Some parts of this poetry sometimes become slogans and add fuel to the fire. This kind of poetry gives vent to sorrows and sufferings although without truth, zest, and feeling. No doubt she inflames the national pride but that is ephemeral because the characteristic of a slogan is that it will subside soon, and the zeal will be severed after lightening the burden of expression. Anyway Tagore, Dinkar, Iqbal, Bankim Chandra, Prasad, Mehjoor, Azad et al., are poets of the national level and Sarat Chandra, K. M. Munshi, Prem Chand, and others are considered as novelists because in a large body of their writings the past of the country, present, and it is said the future has also been pictured.

Poetry and the novel are not similar to each other only due to their themes, and they are not separate from each other only due to the usage of words and construction of sentences. Their similarities and differences are set up during the process of creation. It is not correct to say that because poetry is limited to the personality of the poet, it cannot transport. And that the novel, because it moves outside the personality of the writer into the conditions and characters, owns a wider circle of rights. The truth is that the novel also springs forth from the personality and the poetry also is born out of the process of reaching outside of the personality of the writer. The fact of the matter is that literary experiments demand honesty and passion, whether it finds expression in poetry or prose. The difference in genre is subject to the external factors of the knowledge and training of the writer. The second person who might be a reader, listener, or a critic is present in the personal process of the creator as well as in the impersonal, adjectival, impressionistic process. The poet speaks after inflicting the suffering of the Other on his person, and the novelist speaks of the pain of the Other in the external context of the latter. That is why the realm of the novelist is found to be wider and that of the poet narrow. That is why the relations of the characters in the novel emerge to be full of suspense and are seen to be mobile and appear to be shrunken inside that of the poet. It is because of the differences in their creation and expression that more than the above-mentioned national poets, the circle of impact and representation appears to be wider in the case of the novelists. If there is only a poet or a novelist, then the separation of genres shows the difference between them; otherwise both of them have the stimulus from the same literary movement.

In literary fiction, the presence of the element of narrative is necessary. This is important in traditional short stories, novels as well as in the modern creative writings. From the point of view of the genesis and the method, it is important to have characteristics of the collective in the short story. The narration moves through the characters and gives their characteristics although the springhead of these characteristics is the narrator himself, just that he has collected several characters in the narrative keeping in view their usage and explanation. A poet appears to be just a sufferer of the experiences and a short story writer as a witness although both are actually possessors of some good quality. Due to the conditions of expression the witnessing and suffering dimensions of the creative writers emerge. It is better that we carry forward this brief discussion onwards from what is noticed first; that is the role of the witness of the short story writer, the characteristics, and the characters.

The witnessing dimensionality of the fictionalist gives him the comprehension to feel in detail the age, the surrounding conditions, and the colourfulness. These details are made available to him by the characters, their psychological traits, and the environment. He conceives in his personality the personalities around him and evokes the probabilities of the conditions. But if there is any limited line of thinking or any deliberate thought process at work in him, then it appears that he is compromised. Even if that has been used because of the compulsions to create speed in the national material or social progress. Literature written under some conditions does not create the reason for the mental liberation of the writer or that of his reader for whom it is planned to be written. Not just literature, any kind of knowledge should be able to open the knots and twists and must encourage the human beings to live like human beings. How meaningful is this old Sanskrit saying, which reflects the wisdom of the thinkers of the yore!:

Sa Vidya Ya Vimuktaye
(Real knowledge is that which liberates)

This is also a fact that the knots and the twists do not take time to take birth in our convoluted society because we are caught up in such a struggle in which each moment is converted into a question and encountering the snares of our existence is routine. In order to survive the snares, skulduggery, and falsehood, we have to wear false faces. Our condition is somewhat like that of Europe two to three hundred years ago. If we keep in view the world history we are still living in the Middle Ages. If most of our intellectual treasure is enclosed and is not opening up, and if our intellectuals are not coming out into fresh air from their narrow cocoons, perhaps the whole blame does not fall on them. Our valley has preserved its special disposition for thousands of years and protected her exclusive rationale of life. However, while protecting this, she shrank and sometimes went on rejecting what came from outside whose proof is available today.

What can be done now when in our collective subconscious we face these dark and bright spots, and our conscious is confronted with the winds of modernity? This wind does not keep the same direction nor has anyone found any end or exit from it. This is an existence on borrowed time in these winds. Should we move around with complaints or with a first aid box? Meaning, should we describe our distressed nation like that of a spectator as in the case of some other professional narrators, should we get along with the new ways of thinking, or should we like that of a self-less litterateur see, understand, and express human being as a human being? It is not difficult to decide.

There *is* separation. By confessing this we testify that there was a bond. The connection encourages my characters to live, although, due to indignation, they become temporarily worried. They indulge in ostentation and then rub their wrists wondering what they have done. They are enmeshed in the net of politics but when they witness a contention between politics and reasonable humanity, they become partisans of humanity. My characters do not wish to continue with bickering but after all they are human beings and not angels. They do not forget to bicker. These are not unswerving men but during unfavourable conditions they unknowingly create miracles. Assembling the torn fragments and by restoring the relationships they show those qualities which even big politicians or social activists cannot do. After all this, I do not claim to be the creator of these short stories. Very humbly, I place this fourth collection of short stories before the skilful and sympathetic readers.